'What do you see when you look at me, Cal?'

He didn't answer for a while. Then he said, his voice hoarse, 'I see the beautiful sister of the beautiful woman my brother was married to.'

It was flattering, but it was not the answer she wanted. 'Think of Helen's face,' she urged, 'and then look again.'

Of course he knew what she was trying to prove. 'There is some…definite resemblance,' he muttered after a while.

'That isn't all. To look at, that child could be mine. I could be her mother.'

Already they were close, but she moved even closer to make her point. And if he was forced to look at her, then she was forced to look at him. The face that could hide so much now seemed to reveal, as if behind the hard muscled cheeks and veiled eyes she could see a truth he was trying to keep hidden.

Suddenly they were not discussing a child. Their eyes were fixed on each other; they spoke in a language deeper than words. Their lips touched, the gentlest of touches.

The GPs, the nurses, the community, the location...

LAKESIDE PRACTICE

A dramatic place to fall in love...

Welcome to **Keldale**, a village nestled in the
hills of the beautiful Lake District...where the
medical staff face everything from dramatic
mountain rescues to delivering babies—
as well as the emotional rollercoasters of their own lives.

Visit Keldale again for practice midwife Lyn's story—
coming soon in Medical Romance™

THE DOCTOR'S
ADOPTION WISH

BY
GILL SANDERSON

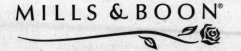

MILLS & BOON®

Dedicated to Pauline Goldstein.
Friend and nurse extraordinaire.

First published in Great Britain 2003
Harlequin Mills & Boon Limited,
Eton House, 18-24 Paradise Road, Richmond, Surrey TW9 1SR

© Gill Sanderson 2003

ISBN 0 263 83426 3

Set in Times Roman 10½ on 12 pt.
03-0203-51238

Printed and bound in Spain
by Litografia Rosés, S.A., Barcelona

CHAPTER ONE

'WHEN the groom proposes the toast to the bridesmaids, he has to say they are beautiful. Then the best man replies on their behalf, and he's supposed to agree. Well, I'm the chief bridesmaid, and when you agree that I'm beautiful, I want you to say it with a smile on your face. As if you mean it. For a best man you're looking very gloomy.'

Jane Hall, now his sister-in-law, had looked at Cal Mitchell with some irritation—he could recall her expression perfectly. And Cal had thought he'd been doing well. He'd stood by his brother, produced the ring, taken Jane's arm as they'd followed the newly married couple down the aisle. What more could she have wanted?

True, so far things had been formal and easy. But then the ceremony had been over and it had been time for the reception. There had been the dinner, the speeches and afterwards a dance in the hotel ballroom. He hadn't been looking forward to it. His speech had been written, he would give it, but as soon as he could afterwards he had intended to quietly disappear.

'Well?' Jane asked.

He looked at her, and at her two tiny companions. 'You are beautiful,' he said. 'All three of you are beautiful.'

Jane picked up the four-year-old smallest bridesmaid and kissed her on the cheek. 'He's a flatterer,' she said. 'I don't think we're going to believe him, are we?'

'I've been called many things in my life, but never a flatterer. Believe me, I mean it.' And he did mean it.

Jane's older sister Marie had just married his younger brother Peter. Traditionally bridesmaids weren't supposed to outshine the bride. No one seemed to have told Jane this. Certainly Marie had been radiant and beautiful and her happiness so obvious that it seemed to move everyone she spoke to. Except himself, of course. But he knew his brother was a very lucky man.

Jane was something else. Her long pink dress made her seem even taller than she was. She had a slim, athlete's body, but with generous feminine curves. And her heart-shaped face was framed in an exuberant mass of blonde curls. He guessed it was the result of a long visit to the hairdresser, but it made her look wonderful.

'So you promise to smile and be happy like the rest of us?'

'Well, I certainly promise to smile.' And he did. Being happy, though, was something else.

That had been four years ago, in Keldale, in the Lake District. And thousands of miles from where he was walking now, high in California's Sierra Nevada.

Stopping for a moment, he leaned his rucksack on a boulder and wiped the sweat from his forehead. He had started early, while it had still been dark. His route covered nine miles, with 4,000 feet of ascent, and he wanted to arrive before the full heat of noon.

This land was awe-inspiring. His trail had led up a valley, passing giant redwood trees. Now he was in open country, and high above him he could see the plateau, where he knew the High Sierra campsite was situated. Around him there were distant blue-grey peaks, one of which was the snow-topped Mount Whitney, the highest mountain on the mainland of America.

He should have been enjoying himself. The scenery was spectacular and the air like champagne. But this wasn't to be a happy trip.

He started to walk on again, a remorseless fast pace that taxed him, bringing pain to his body so that his mind might have some peace. Often it had worked before, perhaps it would work now.

Surprisingly, he found himself remembering the wedding again, that first—and only—meeting with Jane. There was some comfort in the memories—he had felt a little unexpected happiness.

The reception had been held in a country hotel not far from Keldale, the village where they'd all lived. It had been hot—hot like it was now—and the ballroom had opened out onto the gardens so the guests could walk in the open air. For a wedding it had been an ideal day and setting.

He hadn't wanted to be best man. The ruins of his own marriage had been too close, his feelings too bitter. But no way could he have denied his brother's request. So he had performed his duties perfectly, smiled when he'd made his best man's speech, replied to the bridesmaids' toast and agreed they were beautiful. He'd coped, he always did.

But no way had he been going to stay for long after the dancing had started. This hadn't been for him. He'd watched as the newly married couple had taken to the floor and had bitterly remembered how he had done the same two years previously. He'd hoped they would do better than he had done.

Other couples had started moving onto the floor. All had been going well, his duties over. He could slip away, he'd decided.

Then there had been a tap on his shoulder. He had

turned and there had been Jane. Even though he'd thought a woman would never interest him again, his heart had lurched a little. Her face had been alive and she'd been ravishing!

'Not only have you to agree that I'm beautiful, but the best man has to dance with the chief bridesmaid.'

'I didn't know that! It's not in the little book I bought about the best man's duties.'

'It's a well-known tradition that I've just made up. Now, are we going to dance?'

So he danced with her and, much to his amazement, found that he was enjoying himself.

'I saw you were looking grim,' she said, 'and you're not to be grim at my sister's and your brother's wedding. I know you're recently divorced. I'm sorry you made a mistake but this marriage will be different.'

He laughed. 'You don't care what you say, do you?'

'Not if I think I am right.' She looked up thoughtfully. 'You're not mad at me, are you?'

'Well, I could be but I'm not.'

And after that he stayed. It seemed to him to be ill-mannered just to disappear. They found a table together and he fetched them a bottle of champagne.

She told him she was a nurse, at present working in an orphanage in Peru, which was why they hadn't met before. She'd just flown home for the wedding. And she still appeared to know everyone. He had lived nearby until he was eighteen but had hardly returned in the past twelve years, losing touch with everyone except his brother.

And after a quick conversation they danced again. She was a good dancer, and what she lacked in skill she made up in vitality. Against all expectation he was enjoying himself!

Other people came to their table to chat and many of them asked her to dance. She was obviously popular. But she kept on returning to their table. She seemed to like his company. Or perhaps this was what the chief brides-maid was supposed to do. Whatever, he wasn't about to object.

Night fell, but it was still very warm. After a particu-larly energetic dance he invited her to walk out in the garden, where it would be cooler. They slipped out of one of the French windows down the side of the ballroom and walked across the lawn.

There was a rose garden beyond the lawn, heavy with scent. It seemed natural to hold her hand as they saun-tered towards a stone bench. No one else was around. He put his arm round her shoulders when they sat on the bench, and she leaned against him.

'This is so lovely,' she said.

He didn't like to ask whether it was the coolness of the evening air, the wedding or being with him that was lovely. He just said, 'Yes, it is lovely.' Then they both were silent.

In the distance they could hear the sounds of the band, the chatter of the guests. There was the flicker of dancers through the French windows, but they seemed self-contained in their little arbour. He realised he was happier than he had been in months.

He kissed her. Just a friendly kiss really. It was a pleas-ant evening and they had both had a couple of glasses of champagne. It was just the kiss of a brother-in-law for a sister-in-law. Happily, she kissed him back. So then he kissed her again. It was different this time. Suddenly he found it was the kiss of a lover, passionate and demand-ing. He felt her hesitation and then her acceptance of him. Time was suddenly blotted out, there were only the two of them there. Their kiss might have lasted a minute or an hour.

Then their lips parted. It was time to think, to consider. He had never expected this! His iron resolve was weakening, she was so gorgeous!

Her voice was curious. 'Are weddings catching?' she asked. 'Well, not weddings but…you know. I don't usually kiss men so soon after I've met them. Not like this anyway.'

'To tell the truth, I'm as…surprised about this as you are.'

'And you've only just got divorced.'

'No, I'm not divorced. Not really.' It was only a small point. His marriage was truly over. They had started the legal proceedings and the results would follow later.

'What? You're still married?'

He hadn't realised a voice could change so much and so quickly.

'Technically I suppose I am still married. But we've parted. There's no hurry now. I've got better things to do than fall in line with my wife's little whims.'

'And I've got…not better but other things to do than be found kissing a married man. I've enjoyed our walk in the garden, Dr Mitchell, but I'm cooler now. Shall we go back in?'

Yes, she was cooler now. She didn't hold his hand on the way back, and when they reached the ballroom she excused herself and headed straight for the ladies' cloakroom. When he saw her next she was dancing with one of her innumerable friends, smiling as she had smiled up at him. What had he been playing at?

He went to see his brother and new sister-in-law, muttered further congratulations and said he was feeling tired, he would go now. Then, quietly, he left. He should have known better than to be tempted—even a little.

Since that day his hardness had increased. Although there had been a few half-hearted affairs, he had never looked seriously at another woman. And he had never seen Jane again.

She was a wanderer. She took job after job throughout the world. He learned a little of her through her letters to her sister and he was always interested. But somehow they never met on the infrequent occasions when she was home.

Now he was closer to the camp he could see the trail of smoke from the cookhouse—they'd be just having breakfast. Perhaps it would take him thirty minutes to get there; he wasn't looking forward to arriving. The half-pleasant memories he had of Jane were an evil contrast with what he had to say soon. Perhaps he would stop for another rest. Give Jane Hall another ten minutes' happiness.

Jane was happy. She sat on a wooden bench overlooking the great slope that ran down to the river valley far below and then up again to the snow-capped peaks. Travelling, wandering, staying at places like this, this was what she lived for.

It was five years since she had passed her nursing exams, become a state registered nurse, and in that time she had worked in seven different countries. But this job was the best so far, nurse and general instructor at an outdoor camp. She got on well with the other instructors and the clients who needed guidance in having a safe outdoor life. The pay wasn't much—but who cared? She had little to spend it on.

'Brought you another coffee.'

She looked up to see Brad Fields smiling down at her, two mugs of coffee in his hands. She liked Brad. He was a typical cowboy, from the high boots to the large Stetson that he wore even when eating his breakfast. But he was also a great climber—it was what he lived for. At present he was manager of the camp, but she knew that, like her, in time he would be on his way.

There were only four staff in the camp at the moment. In two days' time there would be another gang of green-horns coming up for a fortnight's exposure to the true wilderness. And they would get sunburned, have digestive troubles, cut, scratch and graze themselves, sprain ankles and wrists, perhaps even break the odd bone. A nurse was always needed. But now it was quiet.

'Going down to the big city to pick up a few stores tomorrow,' Brad said. 'Want to come along? We could stay in a motel, perhaps take in a movie or something.'

Brad was a friend, but she knew he wanted things to go further between them. There had been hints, sugges-tions—but all very casual. Brad needed to be casual, it was his style. She would also be casual, she was fine with the way things were between them. She liked to travel light emotionally as well as physically.

'Don't think so,' she said laconically. 'Thanks for the offer, but you go. I'll stay here and mind the shop.'

He accepted her rejection as nonchalantly as he did everything. 'My hard luck,' he drawled. 'But I guess I'll keep on asking.'

'And I'll keep on saying no.' She grinned, sipping her coffee. Life here was good.

Carelessly, she scanned the valley below, then frowned. 'We're going to have a visitor,' she said. Far below them they could see a dot, moving slowly up the trail.

'We're not expecting anyone,' Brad said. 'Wonder who it could be?'

The camp was remote and they got very few casual visitors. Both stared down at the tiny figure below. 'I don't like surprises,' he went on. 'I like things to go just the way I want them to. Guess I'll fetch my glasses.' He stood.

A minute later he returned, a powerful pair of binoculars in his hand. He put then to his eyes and focussed. 'Single man,' he muttered. 'He's moving well, he must be fit. Carrying a small pack. If he's coming here he doesn't expect to stay for long. I don't recognise him.'

'Let's have a look,' said Jane, and took the glasses from him.

The man below had walked into the shadow of a rock, but now he moved out into the sunshine again and she could see him quite clearly. It was the walk she remembered first of all. Long-paced, easy, as if the man could have walked for ever. But the casual-looking movement was deceptive. When he wanted to, this man could move fast.

The last time she had seen him he had been wearing a grey morning suit, a white shirt and a cravat. He had looked well in the outfit. But now he looked even better, in cord climbing breeches and thin shirt. She could see the ends of the slightly long dark hair escaping from under his cap. She remembered that generous mouth, too often held tight, and the incredible blue eyes.

She remembered him well, and over the years she had often thought about him. He had affected her more than she'd wanted to acknowledge, which was ridiculous. He was just an acquaintance to her. 'I know him,' she said. 'His name is Cal Mitchell.'

'Friend of yours?' Brad's voice was as casual as ever.

'Yes...well, no...he's my brother-in-law. Double brother-in-law really. His brother married my sister.'

'Sounds complicated. You expecting him?'

'No, not at all. I wonder what he's doing here.'

'We'll both soon find out. You don't seem to know if he's a friend or not?'

Jane thought. 'I've only met him once, but I think I liked him then. At my sister's wedding.' She considered. 'I was younger then, I think I was a bit of a prig. He was going through a messy separation and we were getting on fine until he told me he wasn't exactly divorced yet. So I told him I wanted nothing to do with a man who was still married. And ten minutes later he was gone.'

'Sounds like a touchy type,' Brad said.

'No, I was the touchy type. It was just that I'd had...dealings with a man who hadn't told me he was married. Anyway, I've had letters from my sister since then, and she likes him a lot. I think I misjudged him.' Jane paused a minute and when she spoke again there was just a touch of unease in her voice. 'I wonder what he's doing here.'

Cal reached the camp half an hour later. For the last quarter of an hour he had known he was being watched, and for the last ten minutes he had been able to make out Jane. She had waved to him enthusiastically, he had managed to wave back. A little.

He knew his pace was slowing and forced himself to walk faster. Then, all too soon, he was stepping onto the little plateau, seeing the neat ranges of tents, the cookhouse, the benches and tables outside. And Jane rushing to meet him.

'Cal! It is Cal, isn't it? It's good to see you. Why didn't you let me know that you were...?'

Then she got near enough to see his face closely, to
read what he knew must be there. 'Cal? Cal…?' Her
voice rose to a scream. 'What is it, Cal? Why are you
here?'

He took her arm, knowing there was nothing he could
say that would help. But he had to say it. 'Is there somewhere where we can sit down? Be alone?'

A bit of his mind told him that he had travelled so
many miles to put himself through this agony, and he
hadn't needed to. A letter would have reached her in
time. There was no phone up here, and the radio was a
bit uncertain… No, he had needed to come.

She had led him to a tent, obviously hers. He could
see her few possessions, the rucksack at the head of the
bed. On a bedside table there were photographs, including one of herself in her bridesmaid's dress, smiling with
her sister and his brother. Suddenly there was something
sticking in his throat.

There was no easy way of saying this. He shut his
eyes. He had rehearsed this speech a dozen times coming
up the mountain but there was still no way of saying it.

But finally… 'Marie and Peter—your sister and my
brother—were both killed in a car crash ten days ago.'

Cal was sitting white-faced outside the tent when Brad
found him. There were sounds of frenzied sobbing from
inside the tent. Brad moved to enter but Cal stopped him.
'Not now. She needs some time to herself.'

Brad studied him a moment. 'You don't look so good
yourself. Come on over to the cookhouse and I'll fix you
some breakfast.'

Cal hadn't realised he was hungry. But the vast fry-
up, served on one of the wooden benches outside the
cookhouse, was very welcome and he had to admit that

he felt better—just a little—after he had eaten. Brad had remained silent during the meal, quietly stacking dishes. When he saw Cal had finished he came to sit opposite him. He said, 'Jane and me are good pals. Good pals is all, though I'd like it to be more. If you want to tell me, perhaps I can help in some way.'

Cal looked up. He had quite taken to this tall man, who seemed to have a genuine regard for Jane. 'You know she's my sister-in-law?'

'Yes. She told me that.'

'In fact, we've only ever met once, at the wedding. We seemed to get on at first, we liked each other, but then we had a row. A silly thing. It was my fault. Anyway, Jane was desperately fond of both her sister and my brother. And ten days ago they were both killed in a car crash.'

'Poor kid. I figured it was something like that—but not that bad. She's talked about her family a lot.'

The two men were silent for a while. Then Cal went on, 'I tried to get in touch with her so she could come to the funeral. But it just wasn't possible.'

'We're a bit isolated up here,' Brad agreed.

'And after the funeral I just couldn't bear to think of her getting the news from a letter. So I took a few days off work and came to find her myself. Now I'm the only relation she has left—almost.'

'Almost?' Brad asked, puzzled.

The two men jerked round as an unsteady voice spoke from behind them. 'There's a little girl left. Helen Jane Mitchell. My niece, named after me. She's three and she's an orphan.'

The two stood as Jane came to the bench. Cal looked at her white face and the red-rimmed eyes and his heart went out to her bravery. She tried to control her voice but it was unsteady. She sat and said to Cal, 'I want to know all about it. I want every last detail.'

Brad said, 'You two sit here and I'll fetch you more coffee.'

'Typical cowboy. Thinks every problem will be solved by coffee,' Jane said with a desperate attempt at humour.

Brad rested his hand on her shoulder a moment. 'It always helps me,' he said. 'Now, I'll leave you two alone, you have plenty to talk about.' He frowned. 'Just one thing. Jane, if you want to leave, I'll be sorry but that's fine. I can pick up someone to take your place tomorrow.'

She nodded. 'Thanks Brad. That's good of you.' And then he was gone.

Cal didn't know what to say. He looked at the distraught girl in front of him, and thought that even though she was so distressed she was still lovely. The hair he remembered as a cascade of golden curls was now tied back, the pink bridesmaid's outfit replaced by jeans and a red tartan shirt. But she was still lovely. Still—these thoughts were out of place.

'Tell me now,' she said. 'Not everything, just what I need to know.'

So he told her, and watched the tears flow again. Brad drifted up silently, left a pot of coffee and two mugs and went away without speaking. Cal wondered if he should say how sorry he was—but decided she knew that anyway.

'It was good of you to come to tell me in person,' she said after a while. 'I just couldn't have coped if I'd received a letter.'

He nodded. 'It was something I wanted to do. You were out here, with no relations, and I didn't know about friends…and there's also something we have to discuss.

I really need to talk to you about Helen. She's no one left in the world now and, of course, she's living with me. I want to adopt her.'

Jane looked at him then, and he could see an alert mind working through the tears. 'Helen has got someone else left in the world,' she said. 'She's got me.'

'Well, of course. I would expect you to—'

She interrupted him. 'I suggest you go to my tent and try to get some sleep for a couple of hours. Then, if you're up to the reverse walk, we'll leave this place this afternoon. I'm coming back to England with you.'

He looked at her. He hadn't expected this. 'But haven't you—?'

'I can pack in half an hour, I always travel light. Are you fit enough for the walk back?'

This irritated him a little. 'Yes, I'm fit enough.'

'Well, go and sleep for a while.'

'I'll rest,' he said, 'but there's no way I'll sleep. Can I do anything else for you?'

'Who can do anything for me now?' He could hear an infinity of desolation in her voice.

Jane walked to the far edge of the camp, to a little outcrop where she could weep again if she wished. She knew Brad would only come to speak if she asked him, and she needed to cope with her grief alone.

The initial shock was now wearing off and this made the news even harder to bear. Suddenly there was a great emptiness in her life. Things she had been certain of, had never questioned, had disappeared. She thought of the few times she had visited her family, had sat with her niece on her lap, having a chat with her sister. She could have seen them so much more! Instead, she had roamed the world, gone her own way. Now she was finding that her own way wasn't enough, and she felt lonelier than she had ever felt in her life.

It was good of Cal to come in person to tell her. She wondered how he was coping. He appeared to be in control of his feelings. But, then, Marie had written saying that Cal always coped. He seldom went out with other women, was still bitter about his divorce. 'Like you,' Marie had written, 'he seems to be completely self-contained.' Self-contained! If Marie could see her now! But, then, Marie was… Jane was racked with sobs again.

She stared around her, tried to draw some comfort from the wilderness, the view of distant plains, forests, peaks. Usually, whatever the problem, this calmed her. But not today.

What was she to do? She had to go back, of course. She had to say her own goodbyes. But then?

'Jane? Jane? Are you there, Jane?'

It was Brad calling her, but not in the caring, thoughtful tones he had used before. This time his voice was more brusque. This was business. She rubbed her face, stood and turned to him. 'Trouble, Brad?'

'Trouble,' he confirmed. 'Couple of walkers have just staggered into camp. They're walking the ridge, been doing it for three days. One of them, the girl, had a fall about an hour ago, split her head open on a rock. They dumped their kit and the man just managed to drag her here. There's blood everywhere, Jane, I've never seen so much blood. I dunno whether to call in a chopper or not.'

Jane had her troubles but this was work. 'Let's take a look,' she said.

The girl was on one of the benches by the cookhouse, slumped against the shoulder of the man. He had his arm round her, and Jane could see his anxious face. The girl clutched a scarf to her bleeding head and, as Brad had said, there was blood everywhere.

'It's all right,' Jane said gently. 'You're with friends now and we'll soon see you're all right. I'm Jane. What's your name?'

'She's Angie,' the young man said quickly. 'She's Angie and I'm Derrick. Can you stop the bleeding? She can't go on like this.'

'Just let me have a look. I won't hurt you,' Jane said, and gently pried the fingers away from the cut. It was deep and long, stretching from the top of the skull down across the forehead to the top of the right eye. But the bleeding appeared to be slowing now. To carry on walking had not been the right thing to do. Ideally, Angie should have rested until help came. But up here in the wilderness help was hard to come by.

'Take her into the cookhouse and get her to lie on one of the benches,' Jane said. 'I'll get out the medical supplies. Brad, you go and wake Cal Mitchell.'

'Cal? What can he—?'

'He's a doctor,' Jane said, and derived a little satisfaction from Brad's expression of surprise.

Before fetching the medical kit Jane washed her hands and splashed cold water on her face. Then she dragged the two great boxes into the cookhouse, just as Brad arrived back with Cal.

She saw Cal's eyes flick to her, register that she could work. No longer were they a bereaved brother and sister. Now they were doctor and nurse.

'Angie's had a fall,' she explained. 'She's had to walk for the past hour. Now, this is our medical kit—it's quite a good one.' She opened the two boxes and showed him the list of contents fastened to the inside of the lid. She had been in mountain schools previously where the idea of a medical kit was a bottle of aspirins and a roll of sticking plaster. This kit was different, and had been compiled with efficiency. There were supplies to cover the most extreme of emergencies.

Cal glanced at the contents, then said, 'I think we'll start by cleaning Angie up a bit. Could you get a bowl of warm water, Jane?'

They got to work. Jane washed Angie's face and then cut away a little of her hair as Cal made a quick inspection of the rest of her body, checked Angie's eyes for signs of concussion. It was too easy to overlook a minor but still life-threatening injury. Then they rigged up an intravenous drip as Angie had lost too much fluid. When they could see the full extent of the injury, Cal started the difficult task of anaesthetising the area round the cut. This wasn't going to be easy.

Jane had done some suturing herself, in one or two cases having been the only person available. She had also watched while surgeons tacked together horrific wounds. So she knew how hard this could be. And Cal was good! Patient, expert, he was a pleasure to watch.

Eventually he was finished. He gave Angie a sedative and she was found a bed to sleep in. 'All this way to practise medicine,' he said with a grin.

'I'm sure glad you were here,' Brad said when they had finished and were having yet one more mug of coffee. 'I know nothing about surgery but that stitching you did looked a really good job. Could you have done as well, Jane?'

'I could have done some sort of job,' she said, 'and I would have tried, 'cos that wound needed closing. But I'm not as good as Cal.'

'I've done a lot of suturing,' Cal said simply. 'In my

practice there seem to be a lot of people who cut themselves. Farmers more than mountaineers, probably.'

'Well, I thank you,' Brad said. 'Cal, I'll give you the address of our head office. If you send in a bill, I'll see it gets paid.'

Cal shook his head. 'Have this one free. I won't send a bill.'

Brad looked at him, perplexed. 'You did the job, you're entitled to be paid. Insurance will cover it.'

Cal shrugged. 'I'm well enough paid at home. And I don't practise medicine because of the money. I do it because I like it.'

'Whatever you say,' Brad said.

CHAPTER TWO

'THAT pack is too heavy for you. Let me carry it.'

'No. This is my stuff. I carried it up here, I'm going to carry it down.'

Jane could tell Cal hadn't expected her to object. He didn't know her very well.

'Well, let me carry half of it. That way we'll move a lot quicker.'

This was quite a reasonable idea but she still had no intention of agreeing. 'The contents of this rucksack are all I have. They're my life. I like to be able to carry all I need on my back.'

'So carrying the rucksack is some kind of statement about life?' They were about to set off on the long walk and they were arguing already.

'You could say that.'

He looked at her a moment and then said, 'I think I understand. But I carry all the water. And promise me that if it gets too much for you, you'll tell me.'

This she could agree to. 'No problem. I'm not stupid.'

They knew it wouldn't be good to walk through the heat of the middle of the day, and as they dropped down into the valley it would get even warmer. So they waited until it was late afternoon. Then she hugged Brad, said goodbye and promised to keep in touch. And she and Cal set off down the trail.

Cal had worried about her, and at first she had worried about him. It was a long trek to come up to the camp and then go back on the same day. But she had seen the efficient way he walked, noted the lean figure and the muscles showing through the thin shirt and breeches, and guessed he would manage.

After five minutes he said, 'I'm happy just to walk, but if you feel the need to talk, that's fine.'

'Which would you rather do?'

He shrugged. 'Over the past few days there's been nothing much I wanted to say to anyone. I suppose that will change.'

'I suppose so, in time. I might…I might ask you to walk on a bit, leave me alone for a minute or two.'

'That's fine. I understand the need to be alone.' After that they walked in silence.

There was some kind of relief in having to work so hard. Jane consciously pushed her body so that the physical pain stopped the grief. But it wouldn't work indefinitely. After a while the tears came, and she just couldn't walk on. She stopped. Cal looked at her and she could see the understanding and concern on his face. But they both knew that there was nothing he could do or say. Silently, she shook her head and he walked on a hundred yards and waited for her there.

In time she felt not better but less bad, so she wiped her face with the bandanna round her neck and walked up to him. He said nothing but offered her the canteen of water. She drank deeply, and then they walked on.

It was dusk and three hours later when they got to the trail head. There were half a dozen cars parked there, Cal's hired car among them.

'I've got a motel room waiting for me,' he said. 'I reserved one for you just in case.'

'Just in case?'

'I thought there'd be a small chance you'd want to come with me. If you could.'

'You were right. Where's the motel?'

'It's in the next big town, in the valley. Only fifty miles away.'

They loaded their rucksacks into the car and he drove off. He didn't turn on the radio, still disinclined to talk. For a while Jane stared at the half-seen outlines of the mountains around her, glancing at the very occasional light. And then she slept.

She woke for a moment when they turned off the twisty mountain road and Cal accelerated along one of the flat, straight roads that crossed the San Joaquin valley. She half opened her eyes and caught a glimpse of his profile against the night sky. Then she closed her eyes and slept again. There was something comforting in that stern face. Dimly she felt that for a while she could relax. All too soon they would stop again and she would have to wake to the harshness of life. But for the moment she could leave things to Cal.

Their car rolled into the forecourt of the Valley Motel and stopped outside the office. Jane woke to see the pink neon sign high above her. When Cal walked round and opened her door she felt the heat of the night wash over her. Up in the mountains it had been warm, but the air had been fresh. Here in the valley it was hot. For the past half-hour they had needed the car's air-conditioning, and she would switch it on in her room that night.

It was half past nine. 'Are you hungry, Jane?' he asked.

Now he had asked, she realised that, yes, she was hungry. Her last meal had been breakfast. In spite of Brad's prompting, she had been unable to eat more. 'I'm ravenous,' she admitted.

'Good, so am I, and there's quite a good Tex-Mex café round the corner. I'll book us in for the night and then I need to shower and change. Just wait here and I'll go and get the keys.'

She was allowing him to make all the decisions, she noticed. Well, this was fine so far—she felt so emotionally battered that she wanted to think as little for herself as possible. But it wasn't to last. She was her own woman, she would decide what was best for her. Perhaps she ought to show him this.

It was a typical motel room—clean, pleasant, without much character—like a hundred others she had been in. But it was good to have a really powerful shower and to wash her hair. Up in the camp the showers had been cold, and erratic to say the least.

She dressed in clean underwear, blue shorts and a white T-shirt. Casual wear was the thing around here. Then she went out to meet him—having been exactly the twenty minutes they had agreed on. He too had changed, into tan chinos and a similar white T-shirt. He looked at her approvingly.

'You know the right dress for this weather.'

'I've been here a while,' she said laconically. 'D'you realise that it's only a hour's drive and you can be above the snow line?'

'America, land of contrasts. Mind you, the weather has fooled me at home in the Lake District.'

'Don't I remember it.'

They were quickly seated in the restaurant and she sipped the glass of iced water that was automatically put in front of her. When he asked for her local knowledge she suggested they have a bowl of chilli each, with crackers and a pitcher of beer. The meal came, and it was wonderful. They ate first, and when they felt better, they talked.

'I like this place,' he said, looking round approvingly. 'It was a great meal and I like your company. Under different circumstances I could be enjoying myself.'

'Me, too. But…things aren't different. I was very tired. The walk and the news combined—they took it out of me.'

'I know that. How I know it.'

His face looked haunted, and for a moment she realised what he must have been through. All the trauma she had suffered had been his, too, plus he had been on the spot. There must have been arrangements to be made, decisions… She didn't want to think about it. Not tonight.

'We'll talk more in the morning,' he said. 'But it would help if I knew roughly what your plans were.'

What were her plans? She had no real idea. She just knew that she had to get home, to re-establish contact with the place and the people she had been born amongst.

'I'm not sure about long-term plans,' she said. 'I've never really had any. I've always been a wanderer, but there's always been a home for me to come back to. Now my sister and her family are gone…it feels as if my roots have been torn away.'

'There's a lot of your friends left,' he pointed out. 'Not to mention Helen. And you'll always be welcome to come and stay with us, to see her.' He thought a moment and then said, 'I've got a return ticket from Los Angeles to Manchester, there's a good flight tomorrow night. Shall I see if I can get you a ticket on the same flight? I'll get one with an open-ended return.'

'That'll be good of you. But just get a single, I'm not sure of my future plans.'

Cal frowned. He hadn't expected this. Now things were going to be difficult, but they had to be said. Jane went on, 'There are two things—no, three. First of all, I'm so grateful that you came in person to tell me. I couldn't have coped with just receiving a letter.'

'It would have hurt but you'd have coped. You're a coping person.'

'Perhaps. The second thing is that I'm glad to travel with you, but I'll pay for my motel room and my flight back and any other expenses. I've always been independent and I'm going to stay that way.'

He looked at her calmly for a while and then said, 'Admirable, I'm sure. And what's the third thing?'

'The third thing is Helen. It's good of you to offer to adopt her. But she has two blood relations left, you and me. We have equal responsibilities and rights, and I'm not going to duck mine. We deal with Helen together.'

He scowled. 'Above all, Helen now needs security. She needs to know that there's a loving home and that things won't change—people won't disappear. I can provide that security. Judging by past form, you can't. So it's better if I adopt her.' After a moment he added, 'And a bit to my surprise, I like having her live with me.'

There was a lot more she had to say, many more arguments to put forward. She felt the anger rising in her—but also a renewal of the grief. For a moment she was incapable of speech. Once again, she knew that tears were trickling down her face. His stern face suddenly became sympathetic. He reached over to squeeze her hand.

'You've had an awful day, Jane,' he murmured softly.

'Believe me, I know, I've been through it. Why don't we leave any talk until tomorrow? You need to rest.'

For a moment, they held each other's gaze.

'All right,' she said quietly. 'Shall we go now?'

Somehow, Jane slept. In the mornings the sun had shone through the canvas of her tent up at the camp; by comparison, the motel room was completely dark. She was still asleep at eight when Cal knocked on her door.

'Sorry,' she mumbled, peering round the edge of the door. 'Guess I overslept.' She wasn't going to invite him in. Her hair was a mess and she had slept in a thin, short T-shirt. It did little to conceal her. By comparison, he seemed fresh and alert. He had shaved, the darkness had gone from his jaws and cheeks. She could even catch the fragrance of a lemony after-shave. He seemed… well…incredibly attractive.

He handed her a plastic cup. 'Have a cup of coffee. That place we went to last night serves breakfast—how about we go there? Meet here in half an hour? Three quarters?'

'Twenty minutes will be fine,' she said, reaching for the coffee. 'And thanks for this.' No way was she going to let him think she was holding him back!

She showered and then looked gloomily at her rucksack. The trouble with travelling light was that she carried only the bare minimum. And she wanted to make just a little more effort than she had the night before. From a side pocket she dug out a rolled-up summer dress, sleeveless and light blue and guaranteed to be of some creaseless material. Hastily she pulled it on. Well, it was without creases—almost. Perhaps, as she wore it, the few creases there were would drop out.

A pair of quite pleasant white sandals and a touch of make-up completed the look. After all, this was the first time she'd worn a skirt in over three months.

She left her room with one minute to spare of the twenty she'd promised to be. Cal was there waiting for her, staring at the distant grey line of mountains. He turned and she could tell his expression was appreciative. 'You look good,' he said. 'Much more like the girl I met at the wedding.'

'I'm still the same girl underneath,' she said. Their meeting at the wedding came back to her, how for a while they had got on so well together, how she had rebuffed him. They gazed at each other speculatively. She knew that he was also thinking of what had happened then. And both of them decided not to carry on with that train of thought.

Brusquely, he said, 'I'm sure you are. Incidentally, I am now thoroughly, properly and happily divorced. We'll not mention it again, OK?'

'Whatever you wish. But I did know. Marie wrote and told me.' After that there didn't seem to be much more to say on the subject.

The minute they sat down the waitress filled their coffee-cups, fetched the ever-present glasses of iced water. Cal looked at the menu and then at Jane. 'What is a large and a small stack?' he asked.

Jane giggled. 'Pancakes,' she said. 'You eat them with cream and maple syrup. Go very well with bacon and eggs.'

'You wouldn't joke with an old man, would you?' he asked plaintively.

'Live dangerously, try them. I think they're wonderful.'

So, doubtfully, he ordered a small stack. And when he had finished it he said he wished he'd had a large stack.

'Another convert to American country cooking,' Jane said smugly. 'I'm a good pancake-maker myself.'

'You're a woman of many parts, Jane. You're constantly surprising me. Perhaps we...'

She never knew what he was going to say. The waitress leaned over the table, gave him a beaming smile and asked, 'Shall I fill you up, honey?' Jane's coffee-cup was also filled, but with a smaller accompanying smile. And Cal decided to return to business.

'I phoned the airport this morning, we're both booked on a flight out of Los Angeles at seven this evening.'

'Good. There'll be no trouble in reaching L.A. by then. But you won't have much chance for a look around. Wouldn't you have liked to see more of America?'

'Very much so. But I also have to get back to Helen. Perhaps next year I'll come back out here, I might even bring Helen if I can. I'd like to see more of this area, too. Perhaps we could meet up again, do a couple of walks?'

Jane thought about this. 'If I'm back here,' she said cautiously.

He smiled. 'Thinking of another country? Somewhere even more distant, even wilder? Alaska perhaps?'

'Just thinking in general. I have responsibilities now. Perhaps we'll be neighbours in Cumbria.'

This didn't seem to be the best news he had ever heard, but he obviously decided not to comment. 'I also phoned home before you got up. It was early afternoon there and I said hello to Helen. I'm quite missing her.'

'I would have liked to talk to her, too!'

'You can tomorrow. I did think of waking you, asking

you if you wanted a word. But I don't want her being disturbed by people she perhaps doesn't remember. At the moment she needs calm, reassurance. And as I said, you can talk to her tomorrow.'

'I can appreciate your concern,' Jane said. 'But remember, I'm as much her guardian as you are.'

'As you wish.' He looked at her thoughtfully, but said nothing.

They set off on the long drive shortly afterwards. She tried to pay for her motel room, told him she had money. He said he had more. Eventually they agreed that he would pay for her travel, but present her with a detailed bill when they got back to England.

'I mean to pay,' she said firmly. 'In fact, I've got to pay. I'm my own person, I value my independence. I want to be obliged to no one.'

'Everyone needs someone at some time, Jane,' he said. 'I know that sounds like the words of a sentimental song, but it's the truth.'

She didn't know how to answer him.

They drove to the Interstate 99, the great road that ran down the centre of the fertile San Joaquin valley. It was hot, the sunlight shimmering off the concrete ahead as they slid past great articulated trucks carrying fruit and vegetables to the markets of Los Angeles.

'A big country,' he commented. 'You could never see it all.'

'I know. Perhaps that's why I still have a soft spot for Cumbria.' After that they drove on in silence. And after an hour the tears started again. He said nothing, merely offered her a handkerchief.

'I'm sorry,' she mumbled. 'I can't seem to help it. I know you think it's silly and female and—'

'I think nothing of the kind,' he broke in. 'I think weeping is a good and necessary part of the grieving process.'

'Is that so? I can't see you crying like a baby!'

'You're right, I didn't,' he said.

After that they drove on in stony silence. Why does he have to be so hard? she wondered. Hard on me as well as himself. Every now and again I can see a kinder, a more gentle man. But then he disappears. I wish I knew who the real Cal was.

After three hours Cal drew in to buy petrol and collect a couple of cups of coffee which they placed in the holders in the car. And she decided that carrying on like this was silly—they had to speak to each other. She offered to drive, but he said that unfortunately she wasn't insured and thanked her for the offer. After that, things got easier.

They were nearing Los Angeles now, still passing through open countryside but the traffic was building up. 'We'll be there too early if you're not careful,' she said. 'Would you like to turn off into Los Padres National Forest? You must be tired after the past few days. You could have a rest.'

'Good idea. Any suggestion as to where we turn off?'

So she directed him away from the main road to an entrance she had visited before. It was now well into the afternoon so she got him to stop at a shop and went in to buy soft drinks and a couple of filled rolls. Then they drove to a quiet spot surrounded by wooded hills and ate at a table in a picnic area.

'I needed that,' he said when they had finished. 'Now I think I need a quick sleep. We have time, don't we?'

'We have time,' she agreed. 'You're like all the doctors I know. Sleep whenever they can.' She thought for a minute and went on, 'I suspect that you've not had much sleep over the past few days, have you?'

'No. I had a funeral to arrange, a room to decorate for Helen. I wanted to do it myself. And there was still the practice to run.'

She noticed that he talked of work, not about his own feelings. 'So why did you come out to find me?'

He shrugged. 'At first I tried to get in touch with you by telephone. It wasn't easy. The man in your head office said he could get a message to you—but he wasn't sure when. And if it was to be too late for the funeral, I didn't want you to be told by someone who didn't know you and hadn't understood my message. So I took a few days off, flew into Los Angeles, hired a car and came out to look for you.'

'Just to tell me. That was so kind of you.'

'I didn't want you going through what I had gone through, and so far from home. Perhaps I needed a break as well.'

'You haven't had much of a break.' She yawned. 'You know what? I think I'm a bit tired, too.'

'Then we can sleep together.' He reddened. 'Sorry, didn't mean that.'

'I know what you meant.'

They went to the car, reclined their seats and Cal was soon asleep. Sleep came harder to Jane, although she was weary. She looked down at him. As so often happened the harshness in his face disappeared when he was asleep. She could see a younger, less tormented man—a happier man? He had wonderfully curved lips, she noticed. Lips that… Then he stirred in his sleep and she lay back, not wanting him to wake and see her looking down at him, perhaps guess what she was thinking. A moment later she slept herself.

Jane woke first, after an hour or so, and gently eased herself out of the car without disturbing Cal. First she washed her face in the little cloakroom nearby and then went over to the machine by the park entrance and fetched another two plastic cups of coffee. She tried to be quiet as she opened the car door, but he spoke, still with his eyes shut.

'I didn't hear you, you know,' he said. 'It was the smell of the coffee that woke me.'

'Something I like about America. You always seem to be able to get a coffee, wherever you are.'

'I like it, too.' They sat side by side, drinking, apparently at ease with each other. He said, 'We don't have to drive on yet, and I like it here. I'd rather talk among trees than somewhere surrounded by traffic and buildings and smog.'

'Me, too. But what are we going to talk about?'

'I want to talk about the future, not the past. What we have to do together.'

'Our future? Yours and mine?'

He looked vaguely irritated. 'Not yours and mine. Yours, mine and Helen's. I know that you love Helen, and that you're as much her relation as I am. In fact, we're her only two blood relations, although she has plenty of friends.'

'So we look after her together?'

'Well, sort of. I know you want to do what's best for your niece and, as I said, you'll always be welcome to come and stay, for as long as you like. But you're a wanderer. So I want to adopt Helen. I'm sure you'll agree that's the best thing for her.'

In fact, Jane didn't agree at all. But, although she desperately wanted to, for the moment she didn't object out loud. 'Let's think about it,' she suggested. 'You love her, I know that. But you're a man, a bachelor with a very demanding job. How will you look after a small child?'

He smiled, rather smugly, she thought. 'I knew you'd say that. Do you remember a girl called Miriam Watts?'

Jane thought a minute, then frowned. 'Yes I remember a Miriam Watts,' she said. 'She's a couple of years older than me. We went to the same school and then we trained in the same hospital at Leeds, though we didn't see much of each other. A good nurse, tremendously intent on getting on. Not much of a sense of humour, though.'

'You don't really need a sense of humour for the job I have in mind for her.'

Cal laughed, but without much humour himself.

'She got married, didn't she?'

'So she did. And, like me, she got divorced. Apparently from some no-good male nurse who just wouldn't work. Now we both have the same view of marriage.'

In fact, Jane had known the man in question and didn't agree with Cal's description of him. She thought that Miriam had picked the man because she hadn't been able to land one of the doctors she had been angling for. But then…she would keep quiet for a while longer. She needed to listen before she could object.

'Well, carry on,' she prompted.

'Miriam is now a charge nurse in a pediatric ward in a large London hospital. She likes the work but not London. I've seen quite a bit of her recently as she often comes up to visit her parents. Anyway, I've offered her a job as live-in nanny and housekeeper.'

Jane thought for a minute. 'Just exactly how close have you been to her?' she asked. 'If you don't mind me asking, of course.'

She turned to see his face darken. 'Our former relationship is no business of yours,' he snapped. 'There's nothing between us now.'

'I see,' said Jane, thinking that she saw very well. 'You know that she wants to marry you, don't you? Once you've got her in the house you'll never get her out. She'll marry you. I know her.'

'That's ridiculous! I've been married once and so has she, and the one thing we're agreed on is that marriage is the last thing we need.'

'So you've talked about it. That's a start anyway.'

She could tell he was trying to hold onto his temper. 'It's the start of nothing. This is a purely business arrangement. Miriam wants to come back to the North and be near her parents. She's an excellent paediatric nurse, and will make a fine nanny for Helen.'

'Helen needs more than a paediatric nurse! She needs a mother.' Now Jane was getting angry, too.

'Helen's mother is dead!'

Jane knew he hadn't meant to say it. He wasn't a cruel man. But the words hung between them in the car, simple and stark, and once more she felt the pain threaten to choke her.

'I'm sorry,' he said quietly after a moment. 'I didn't mean to say that, it was hurtful and unnecessary. Please, forgive me.'

Jane took a deep breath. 'There's nothing to forgive. What you said is true, and we can never forget it.

And…and I do know that you've lost a brother. You've been hurt as much as I have.'

For a while they were both silent. Then, picking her words with care, Jane said, 'I can see that you have thought about this, and you're trying to do the best you can for Helen. But don't you think you should have consulted me?'

'Yes, I do. But you weren't there. As far as I could see, you wouldn't be there in the future. I had to work quickly.'

She had to admit this was fair. 'I can see that, but—'

'No, Jane. The one thing Helen needs now is certainty, security. So, for that matter, do I.'

A bit of her mind registered this last comment, the first time he had mentioned his own feelings.

He went on, 'Helen is a three-year-old child, not a baby. She asks constantly where her mummy and daddy are. And there's no answer. I know you're in the same relationship to her as I am, and you love her, too. You're a loving aunt, and I hope you'll see a lot of Helen. But how many countries have you visited in the past five years? How many weeks have you spent in Cumbria? Come on, tell me.'

Dry-lipped, she counted. 'I've been in seven countries. And I've averaged…perhaps three weeks a year at home.'

'So don't tell me you're going to give up that lifestyle and stay at home. I just don't believe it. Even if you thought you could settle down, I couldn't take the risk with Helen. She must have security.'

'Security! With an embittered bachelor and a predatory housekeeper! Don't make me laugh.'

Then she groaned to herself. She had intended to keep

calm, to show herself a reasonable and thoughtful person. And she'd ruined it. They'd spend the rest of their time together fighting.

But when he spoke again his voice was rueful, amused. 'An embittered bachelor and a predatory housekeeper?' She looked at him, and he was smiling at her. 'What a picture, what a household. Poor Helen!'

Jane struggled. 'Now it's my turn to be sorry,' she muttered. 'Perhaps we're both still in a bit of a state. Perhaps we ought to keep this conversation for a while till we're more…more settled.'

'It might be a good idea. Shall we go?' So she threw away the plastic coffee-cups and they drove out of the park. But as they did so, she was telling herself that the conversation was not yet over, nothing was yet decided. No way was she going to have her niece looked after by Miriam Watts. For that matter, no way was she going to allow Cal to be looked after by Miriam either. He deserved better. This conversation wasn't over by any means.

Shortly after that they entered the vast outskirts of Los Angeles. Cal had to concentrate on his driving more, and as they threaded their way through town after town, and suburb after suburb, she got to admire his calmness and his driving. He was relaxed and confident.

'Do you still think of America as a land of the great open spaces?' she asked.

He smiled, obviously pleased at her change of tone. 'This is nearly as bad as London,' he said.

'Well, do you want me to map-read for you? Perhaps find the way to where you hired the car?'

'No need,' he said cheerfully. 'I memorised the route

this morning. Don't forget, I'm like you, I spend a lot of time in the mountains and I can navigate.'

'This is much worse than any mountain I know.'

But in spite of that he managed to find his way unerringly to where he had hired the car.

After they handed the car in, they were transported to L.A. airport, where they picked up their tickets and made their way through to the departure lounge.

'Feel at home?' he asked. 'Over the years you must have spent many hours in international airports.'

She frowned. 'Usually I like it here. There's that feeling of romance, of knowing there's something different just over the horizon. But today…there just isn't the same buzz. What do you feel?'

'Something like you. It's been a short trip but I've really enjoyed flying out here, walking up and meeting you. But now there are things to do back home.'

Yes, there were things to do back home. She wasn't looking forward to it, and for a moment wondered how Cal felt. Abruptly she said, 'I want to go to the shop, perhaps buy Helen a doll. D'you know if she likes dolls? It's been a while since I saw her.'

'Yes, she likes dolls. For Christmas last year I bought her a teddy bear, she sleeps with it every night.'

Of course, Cal would have seen much more of their niece than she had. He could be very fond of her, she fond of him. Jane wasn't sure of the emotion she was feeling. Surely it couldn't be jealousy?

They went together to the shop, where she bought a native American doll. Once she would have also bought a bottle of spirits for her brother-in-law and sister, but there was no need now… She must stop thinking this way!

She walked rapidly out of the shop and they found seats where they could watch the great variety of planes landing and taking off. She needed to occupy her mind, to think of the things that needed to be done. 'What arrangements have you made in England?' she asked.

Cal seemed to respond to her clipped question, to her need to be businesslike.

'My car is in the park at Manchester airport. We'll pick it up, drive straight back home. You'll stay with me, won't you?'

Jane hadn't thought that far ahead. 'Thank you, that would be very good of you,' she said. 'I...I always used to stay with Marie and Peter.'

'The house is locked up but I've got the keys. I'm one of the executors, it'll be up to me to decide...there's a lot of fiddling around with lawyers to come. I've already spoken to the senior partner of Peter's firm, she'll help us with whatever is needed.'

'Good. Just...not soon but some time...I'd like to sleep one more night in the room I used to stay in. There's a lot of my stuff there. For the past few years it's been my only real home.'

'That'll be fine,' he said gently. 'Will you help me sort things out there? It's not a job I'm fancying.'

'Yes, I'll help,' she said. Then she jerked herself back to other problems. 'Where's Helen living at the moment?'

'Well, she's living in my house. I've turned one of the spare bedrooms into her room. At the moment Lyn Pierce is looking after her. She comes after breakfast every morning and stays as long as is necessary. Lyn has been doing a lot of the looking after since...since it happened. She's my practice midwife, she lives just down the road from me. She knows Helen quite well as she used to babysit for Marie. In fact, Helen spends quite a lot of time at Lyn's home. I had to get a locum for her, I just couldn't hand Helen over to someone she didn't know. And I've still got my surgery to run. But Lyn wants to get back to work soon.'

'I hadn't quite realised just what you've had to go through,' Jane said. 'All this organising.'

He smiled bleakly. 'It's what doctors do,' he said. Then the loudspeaker told them that it was time to board.

They took off in the evening, in the heat of a summer night in Los Angeles. As soon as they'd had their meal, they both put on the masks supplied and tried to sleep. Cal slept soundly, but Jane could only cat-nap.

She tried to avoid thinking about the future, about the decisions she would have to make, about what she would face in the next few hours. Her life was going to change. From now on it would centre on her niece. And that meant she would have to deal with Cal. What did she think of him? How would he fit into her life? For that matter, what did he think of her? This was all too much. She just couldn't deal with all these conflicting ideas.

The twelve-hour journey seemed to be soon over. In no time they were making their final descent and she looked out of her window seat to see the shiny wet runway of Manchester airport. It was raining in Manchester—typical. But she was pleased. This was her home.

'Happy to be back?' Cal asked.

'Sort of. In the past I've always been glad to be back. This is where I grew up.'

'So, do you think you'll be off again soon? Some exotic foreign place?'

She refused to be drawn. 'It's possible,' she said, 'but not very likely. I want to see far more of Helen.'

If I see more of Helen, she thought, then necessarily I'll see more of Cal. She found the prospect alarming—but exciting.

Cal's car was a Land Rover, the four-wheel drive necessary in the hilly district around his surgery. They were soon out of Manchester, on the M6, heading north. It didn't take long before they could see the grey line of mountains ahead of them and she saw his rather grim expression relax into a smile. He seemed more relaxed now, he was coming home. He asked her again, 'So now are you happy to be back?'

'Whenever I see those mountains I wonder why I've bothered to go away,' she said honestly. 'They're part of me, I grew up with them. Other than that, I guess I'm a bit apprehensive.'

'Sounds reasonable. I hope…you'll be happy staying with me.'

'I will be. No one could have been kinder to me, Cal. If we disagree about anything—and I'm sure we will—then I want you always to remember that I'm truly grateful for what you've done.'

'Just part of my job,' he said gruffly. 'Anyone would have done it.' But she thought her little compliment had pleased him.

They turned off the motorway, heading across country to Keldale. As they approached it she could feel her emotions churning again. This was where she had been born, had grown up. She loved the place because it seemed to be full of real people, not just tourists.

Cal's car breasted a hill and there in the valley below

her was her home. And his home, too. 'My turn. How d'you feel?' she asked.

'Happy. When I come over this hill, see the lights of the houses below me, then I know I'm home. This is my place.'

So they agreed on something. They dropped down the hill and she shivered. There was the house she had lived in with her now dead parents. Further down was the small estate of new houses where her sister had lived. But there was also a girl she remembered from school walking along the road, and there was the Red Lion where she had taken her family to lunch on occasions she was home. This was a place of memories, some good, some bad.

'Technically I've got the rest of today and tomorrow off,' said Cal, 'but when we get in I'd like to go over my papers for a couple of hours, see how things are going. What would you like to do?'

'See Helen,' Jane said promptly.

'Good idea. She's probably still at Lyn's house, they spend a lot of time there. We'll go home first, you can freshen up and then go straight to see her.'

'Exactly where is home?' she asked. 'It's good of you to offer me somewhere to stay but I—'

'I live at the back of the surgery. Remember it?'

'I do indeed. Old Dr Evans was my GP. I gather he's now retired. Marie told me a bit about the place. You took over from Dr Evans, didn't you? Came here just after my sister's wedding?'

'I did. I was fed up with London, it was good to come back. But I've had to make a lot of changes, they were necessary. Dr Evans was a brilliant doctor but he hadn't moved into modern times. We've enlarged the practice and there are three partners. We have a couple of trainee doctors—sorry, got to call them registrars now. We've got a practice nurse, a district nurse, a midwife and assorted other staff. We're all looked after by the practice manager. We've taken the old building, altered it and built on a new wing. You won't recognise the old place.'

Jane liked Cal's enthusiasm. 'You're obviously proud of what you've done,' she said.

'It needed doing and I've enjoyed doing it. I thought that this year things might settle down a bit and I might take things a bit easier. There's been a lot of work. But then this happened…'

'Yes. This happened.'

She wondered about his account of what he had done. How much had been a refuge, a way of escaping from memories of his disastrous marriage? Well, his patients and the district had benefited. Dr Evans had certainly been a good doctor, but he had been a solo act. He hadn't really seen the need for all the helpers that Cal had.

He went on, 'Remember down the lane there used to be a little terrace of tumbledown cottages?'

'I remember. About a hundred yards from the surgery.'

'Well, we bought them and had them renovated. Now we keep them for staff who want to rent somewhere for a while. Lyn Pierce is in one of them—she's probably taken Helen there now. You can go round and see her there later.'

They were through the village now and he turned into a broad drive. Jane saw pleasant gardens, then the old Victorian house with cars parked to one side and an extra grey stone wing built onto the other. A sign proclaimed KELDALE SURGERY. He drove round to the back. 'Where I live,' he said.

Jane was suffering from jet-lag now, and her body didn't know if it was morning or evening, day or night. Cal had phoned ahead from the airport so that a room could be prepared for her. She had a vague impression of hall and staircase and then she was shown her bedroom door. 'Have a shower or a bath and then come down in half an hour or so,' he said. 'We'll have a cup of tea and make some plans.'

'That'll be fine. Half an hour.'

But she was more interested in the door across the way, the one painted with a large blue rabbit and the words HELEN'S ROOM. 'May I look in?' she asked.

Silently, he opened the door. A pink bed, wallpaper covered with cute cartoon animals. Mobiles hanging from the ceiling, white-painted furniture with more animal stencils, a shelf of dolls. A little girl's dream room.

'You did all this?' Jane's voice was quiet, impressed.

'Yes,' he replied. 'Usually late at night, when I couldn't sleep. I found that it…helped. Helen slept in the other room until it was finished.'

She looked for a moment and then went to her own room.

It was a fine room, with a view of the back garden and a grove of great trees. There was a faint smell of polish, someone had recently cleaned in there. There was an adjoining modern bathroom and towels laid out on the double bed. But the room was completely without character. Nothing like Helen's room. There were no books, pictures. Nothing to show that this was Cal's home. It might have been a room in an expensive hotel.

She decided to have a bath—something she hadn't treated herself to in a month or two. It was good to lie there and soak. Then she rummaged through her rucksack for fresh clothes. She hadn't many left. She would have to go to her sister's house and raid her wardrobe there. But not today.

After half an hour, feeling considerably better, Jane walked downstairs. She walked along the hall, glancing into a dining room and lounge. All were neat, tidy, clean, well furnished. But there was no sign of Cal's personality at all. Jane thought that she had made a bigger impression on her tent in America than Cal had on his home here. But a tricycle in the hall and a bag of plastic toys hinted that somewhere there was a child.

At the end of the hall she found him sitting in a large kitchen. This was as well equipped as the rest of the house, it could have come from an ad in a housing magazine. Pasted to the fridge door was a set of child's paintings, posters held pictures of fruit and numbers, there was a chair in the corner piled high with cushions. Someone was trying to make the kitchen child-friendly.

Cal had also changed and was now in the more formal clothes of a GP. He smiled at her and poured her a cup of tea. 'Is your room comfortable? Mrs Changer does all my cleaning and so on. I leave all that kind of thing to her.'

'It's very comfortable, thank you.' Then she just couldn't stop herself. 'Cal, this is a lovely house, but there's nothing of you in it. No photos, no pictures, no nothing. Helen has made more of an impact on the place than you have. Why?'

He frowned. 'I hadn't really noticed. I just live here. I like having Helen's drawings and so on but...' his voice suddenly hardened '...if the place needs the woman's touch, I haven't got it and I don't need it.'

'I see,' Jane said. This wasn't the time to pursue the matter.

'I just phoned Lyn,' Cal went on. 'She's at home and she's going to give Helen her lunch there in half an hour. I want to see Helen again but perhaps it's best if you see her alone first. Would you like to walk over to eat with her?'

'Very much. I want to, I need to.' Then she paused and said honestly, 'And I'm a bit frightened.'

He didn't reply for a moment, and she sensed that he was choosing his next words very carefully. Eventually he said, 'Helen has had a deeply traumatic shock—losing both parents. We can't know what she is feeling, how she is coping, but I'm sure you will...that is...she doesn't need upsetting further.'

'You mean, don't hug her and cry all over her and make her as miserable as I am?' Jane asked with some anger. 'I have nursed children before, Cal. I know that much.'

'I'm sure you do. But it'll be hard, won't it?'

For a moment there was silence. Then she muttered, 'Yes, it'll be hard. But you've coped, so I will. Tell me more about Lyn Pierce.'

'She's an excellent midwife and a good friend. There's no one else I would have trusted Helen to so readily.' He looked at her broodingly a minute, then went on, 'I'll tell you this because I know she will in time. She's aged about thirty-two. She was married for five years, got pregnant and miscarried the baby. It was a very late miscarriage. Six months after that her husband was killed in an accident on a farm. They were a devoted couple and we were all devastated. This was three years ago.'

Jane was stunned by this story. 'There's tragedy everywhere I go,' she said. 'Is all life like this?'

'Sometimes it seems that way. But happiness is possible, too.'

Jane nodded. 'And Helen's going to get her chance. I'll see to that.'

'We'll both see to it.' He handed her a set of keys. 'Front door. I want you to treat this place as your home till you decide on your future. Please, stay as long as you wish—you'll be very welcome.'

'What will people think?' Jane asked, trying to be a little light-hearted. 'The two of us living together?'

'They can think what they wish. We know how things are, and that's all that matters. Now, I'm going to work in my study. As I said, I'd like to come to see Helen but I think it best if you go alone at first. Be as long as you like. Tell me how she is when you come back and I'll see her later.'

Jane had no excuse for putting it off now. She set off down towards the cottages.

The rain had stopped now, though the sky was still grey. This was the weather of her childhood—she remembered it and she loved it. She had enjoyed the brassy sun of California, but now it was good to be back in this softer light. She felt happy.

There was a lane at the end of the garden. She turned down it and walked along a cobbled path to a terrace of four cottages. She remembered them as being rather tumbledown, now they were well restored and painted a soft white. There were black cast-iron feed-boxes on the walls. One of the cottages seemed to be vacant and the door of the last in the terrace stood open.

The doll she had bought was in a bright yellow bag,

which Jane clutched a little harder. She knocked on the half-open door. After a moment it was pushed open fully, and a little girl stood there, looking at her. She was dressed in a blue top and blue shorts.

'Auntie Jane?' said the little girl after a moment.

'Hello, darling.' Jane smiled. She didn't burst into tears. Somehow.

As ever, there was a great pile of mail waiting for Cal. He skimmed through it, decided that none of it was absolutely urgent. For a while he could sit, on his own, and think. He was home now.

He had to think about Jane—no, all importantly, he had to think about Helen. Jane had rather upset his plans. When he'd set out for America he'd thought that she would realise at once that what he had in mind for Helen was the very best thing for her. He had never considered that Jane would want to be involved so much in Helen's future. That had been his mistake, he recognised it.

But Jane was a wanderer. He couldn't risk Helen getting fond of someone who would leave in a few months. A second heartbreak would be too much for a little girl.

And how would *he* feel? He had to admit to himself that he had really enjoyed Jane's company. She was cheerful, alive, being with her was never boring. He didn't want her to go, he'd like to see more of her.

Then he frowned and reached for his mail. Such thoughts were foolish. He had been let down by one woman. It wasn't going to happen again.

CHAPTER THREE

THE three of them sat round the kitchen table. Jane fed tiny cheese and tomato sandwiches to her niece, and then cut up an apple and an orange for her. She had been given a sandwich of her own, had eaten it without any idea of what it had contained. On the other side of the table sat Lyn, a dark, attractive girl, obviously very much attached to Helen. She seemed very happy to sit there quietly while Jane got to know Helen again.

After the meal there was the presentation of the doll, and then Lyn and Jane were left alone as Helen played, absorbed, in the corner.

'It's been six months since I saw her,' Jane said to Lyn, 'and she's grown enormously.'

'It's this age. They almost change in front of your eyes. On my rounds I see children I remember bringing into the world, and they're welcoming me by name, carrying my bag. It's frightening how life seems to be passing you by.'

Is life passing me by? Jane thought to herself, Am I missing something? I wonder. But to Lyn she said, 'I gather you're not going to help look after Helen so much now?'

Lyn shook her head decisively. 'No, I'm a midwife and I'm needed round here. But this was an emergency and, since I knew Helen, I was only too happy to stand in while Cal sorted things out. We're a big happy family in the practice, there's a lot of give and take.'

'Cal seems very popular,' Jane said. 'But the first time I met him I found him a bit…intimidating.'

'Well, you don't want to cross him. He's very professional. But in general he creates a good atmosphere, he's a team leader and people are pleased to work for him. And he dotes on Helen.'

Trying to be casual, Jane went on. 'Is there any sign of him getting married—you know, providing a mum for Helen that way?'

'No sign at all,' said Lyn. Only a slight quirk of her lips suggested that she thought the question wasn't an entirely disinterested one. She looked over at Helen. 'D'you want to put this little girl to bed now? She usually has a sleep about now. I keep a bed for her upstairs. If Cal is away late she sometimes stays all night.'

Helen was obviously tired but she wouldn't let go of her new doll. Jane carried her upstairs to the back bedroom.

'In a minute you can read her a story,' Lyn whispered. 'She's a good girl, she'll go to sleep quickly.'

For the moment there was the dolly to be undressed and settled by the bear that Cal had given her.

'She's taken to you very well,' Lyn said, still in the same quiet voice. 'Recently she's been a bit upset by so many new people. Understandable, of course. Now, I'll be downstairs if you need me.'

So Jane held a little hand and read a story about bunnies. Big blue eyes closed before the story was finished. Jane stayed kneeling there, pushing aside the curls from her niece's brow. Two tears dropped heavily on the cotton counterpane, but that was all. There was no time now for self-indulgent emotion.

After twenty minutes Lyn came back upstairs and the two of them looked down at the sleeping infant. 'She could be your daughter,' Lyn said. 'There's the same bone structure around the eyes and she's got your mouth, too.'

Jane looked, perhaps with fresh eyes. She had always thought that Helen looked like her mother but, then, people were always saying that Jane looked like her sister. Yes, she could see it now. Helen could have been her daughter. It was an odd realisation and it made her more determined than ever to look after her niece.

They went downstairs and Jane said that she had better be going. There were things that she had to do.

Lyn looked at her thoughtfully, and said, with the frankness of a professional nurse, 'Yes, you do look a bit washed out. I suppose the past few days have been really hard.'

'Very hard,' Jane said with a shudder. 'It's only a couple of days ago that I was happy and carefree, working in California, and... I don't even fully know what happened yet. I tried to ask Cal but I just couldn't take it.' She paused, and then diffidently asked, 'How did he take it?'

She could tell that Lyn was trying to be cautious. 'He took it hard,' she said after a while. 'He had to...to identify the bodies, make all the arrangements for the funeral, try to get in touch with you and still run a busy practice. And he had everybody's help—and nobody's. No one could get through to him. All the way through he showed that iron self-control, so much so that I wanted to scream at him. No one could penetrate that loneliness.'

'You seem very fond of him,' Jane said.

Lyn laughed. 'I know what you're thinking and you're wrong. When my husband died Cal couldn't have been kinder or more helpful. And because of that he'll always be my brother and never anything more.'

Jane flushed a little. 'I'm sorry, it's just that…'

She couldn't help it. She yawned, and Lyn laughed. 'You need some fresh air,' she said.

Jane knew she was going to be jet-lagged, and also knew that the worst thing to do was to sleep early. 'I'd better go,' she said. 'When will I…?'

'We'll be walking back up to the house at about six,' Lyn said promptly. 'I give Helen her tea there—we arranged that because Cal usually has evening surgery. It's interesting that Helen remembered you so quickly, took to you at once. She doesn't do it with everyone. The more friends she has, the better.'

She walked with Jane to the door. 'You know Cal is thinking of eventually having a housekeeper-nanny to look after Helen?' Jane said just before they parted. 'Have you met her?'

'Miriam Watts? Yes, I've met her.' Lyn smiled.

There was something in that smile that told Jane that there was no way Lyn would be drawn out on the subject of Miriam Watts. Right, Jane thought.

It seemed odd to let herself into Cal's house with her own key. For a moment she was tempted to ring the bell. But then she told herself it would be silly. She unlocked the door, walked along the polished floor, glanced in the perfect rooms. Indeed, it was a very nice house. But it didn't feel lived in, there was no stamp of the owner, no impression of personality. Just the occasional sign that a little girl now lived there.

She tapped on the study door. A voice called to her to come in, no need to knock. She hadn't seen inside this room yet and it was a revelation This was different! The one room that he apparently lived in.

There was a large central table, overflowing with books and papers. To one side was a smaller table, covered with sheets of paper and a big box of crayons. Obviously a child's drawing table. There were book-shelves along two of the walls, a beautiful marble Victorian fireplace, now with a spray of roses instead of coals. Helen's pictures were everywhere. And dominating the room, leaning back on a wooden rocking chair with his feet on the table, was Cal.

'You look at home,' she said.

'This is where I live.' He swung to his feet, took papers off the seat of another chair and indicated that she was to sit down.

'I'll bet the cleaning lady doesn't come in here.'

'She does. Mrs Changer puts flowers in here and vac-uums the carpet. But she's under clear instructions never to move a book or touch a paper. I like things to be as I left them.'

'I can see that. Have you been kept busy?'

He pointed to a pile of papers on the table and the now overflowing waste-paper basket. 'Sometimes I think that I'm an administrator, not a doctor,' he said. 'The com-monest ailment of a GP must be writer's cramp. Now, how was Helen?'

'She was lovely,' said Jane. They were both still stand-ing. Deliberately, she moved close to him, her face turned to the window so he could see her clearly. 'What do you see when you look at me, Cal?'

Cal didn't answer for a while. But then he said, his voice hoarse, 'I see the beautiful sister of the beautiful woman my brother was married to.'

It was flattering, but it wasn't the answer she wanted. 'Think of Helen's face,' she urged, 'and then look again.'

Of course, he knew what she was trying to prove. 'There is some…definite resemblance,' he muttered after a while.

'That isn't all. To look at, that child could be mine. I could be her mother.'

Already they were close but she moved even closer to make her point, almost to intimidate him. But if he was forced to look at her, then she was forced to look at him. The face that could hide so much now seemed to reveal much, as if behind the hard, muscled cheeks and veiled eyes she could see a truth he was trying to keep hidden.

Suddenly, they weren't discussing a child. Their eyes were fixed on each other, they spoke in a language deeper than words. Somehow, their bodies were drawn together the last few inches. Their lips touched, the gentlest of touches. She knew that if she drew back now then all would be well. Nothing more would be said, they could carry on as if nothing had happened. But she wouldn't, couldn't, didn't want to draw back.

Now his fingers were on her shoulder, urging her towards him with a hold so gentle a baby could have broken it. She could no more resist than if she had been dragged to him by iron chains.

Jane felt her body so close to his, her breasts against his chest, his thighs touching hers so that…it was as tender a touch as a bird's wing passing. But the spark between them seemed to light an inferno in them both. His lips came down on hers and he clutched her to him with a strength that almost frightened her.

But she felt as he did. She held him equally as hard, straining to him as if their flesh could be moulded into one. And how he was kissing her!

With an instinctive submission her lips parted, letting him taste her sweetness, letting him give and take a pleasure that was a shadow of one far greater. She felt that her mind, her conscience, call it what you would, had now disappeared. Her body was taking over, leading her

down a dangerous path that led to excitement and fulfil-
ment and...

Her body seemed weak and languid. But there was the
hardness of her nipples where they pressed against his
chest. She knew that he, too, was losing control. She
could feel the heavy beating of his heart, the hardness of
him against her thigh. She was both bewildered and en-
tranced, she only knew that—

The phone rang.

For an infinite second they were still, suspended out
of time, no past, no future, only the rapturous present.
Not now, it couldn't, it wasn't right, perhaps they ought
to... Her mind raced but could find no answer. The phone
rang again.

His lips left hers, though he still held her. She heard
him growl something deep within his throat, moan or
curse, she didn't know which. The phone rang again. It
was impossible to ignore.

They released each other, both aware of a moment
gone that might never be repeated. There was a second,
deeper realisation as they looked at each other and then
backed away. What had they been doing?

He reached for the phone and, miraculously, his voice
was calm. How could it be? 'Cal Mitchell here.'

Jane looked round wildly, wondering what to do,
where to go. She managed to babble, 'I'll make us both
some tea.' Then she fled the room.

Ten minutes later she was sitting in the kitchen, her el-
bows on the table. Her mug of tea was clasped in both
hands, her hair wet and spiky from when she had put her
head under the tap.

It had been hard not to go to her room, to cower there
until she felt more in control. But she knew that she had

to face him some time. Things would only get worse if she waited. It had better be now.

Behind her she heard the door click open, Cal's footsteps on the hard floor. She didn't turn round. There was the sound of the fridge door opening, the clink of something. Then he came to sit opposite her on the other side of the table.

He had a bottle of iced water in his hand. He poured some into a glass and swallowed it in one draught. Only then did he reach for the mug she had put handy and pour himself some tea.

'I thought I should cool down before saying anything,' he said.

She was glad he could joke, even if feebly. 'Me, too. I put my head under the tap.'

He drank his tea, looking at her from across the table. She forced herself to meet his eyes. She didn't see the same expression that had been there such a short time ago. Now his eyes were speculative, thoughtful and ultimately hidden. No longer did she know what he felt, what he wanted.

'That shouldn't have happened,' he said.

She was glad he didn't try to take all the blame. 'Perhaps not,' she said. 'It…came as a shock.' She felt there was something to explain, to make clear. 'It was as much my fault as yours.'

He nodded gravely. 'All right, we were both at fault. We've both been under a lot of pressure recently. There's been the emotional shock, the travelling, not having enough sleep. It's not surprising that we should… should…'

'Act irresponsibly?' she suggested.

'Precisely. Act irresponsibly.' He frowned. 'It's not the

kind of behaviour expected of a doctor. I should be able to control myself, control my feelings.'

'And what about nurses?'

'Yes, nurses, too. Now what do we do?'

'We do nothing, there's no need. It was just a kiss between two…two people who are related.' It took all the strength that she had, but she stood, walked round the table and kissed him on the cheek. 'See, there's nothing to it.'

He sat there, unflinching. 'We have an important job to do together,' he said when she had sat down again. 'We have to see to the welfare, the future happiness of our niece. Our personal feelings mustn't be allowed to interfere with that.'

'Our feelings for our niece are personal,' she told him. 'But I'm sure…I hope we can agree on everything that is good for her.'

To her slight surprise he didn't try to argue about them agreeing. Instead, he sat stone-faced, staring through the window as if thinking disagreeable thoughts.

'You know I was married,' he said after a pause, 'and very quickly after that I got divorced. I swore then never to…to get in a similar mess again. Since then I've seen something of a few women. And I've made it very clear from the outset that our relationship was not to be a lasting one.'

'You must be a great deal of fun to go out with,' she said dryly.

'Perhaps not. But at least I try to be honest. The trouble is, too many women take a statement about a relationship as a challenge, not a condition.'

'I see.' Jane wasn't sure what to say next. It seemed that Cal had revealed a lot of himself, and she suspected that he didn't do this to everyone. 'Why are you telling me all this, Cal?'

He frowned. 'Because I don't want you to get the wrong idea about me.'

'Don't worry, I won't. There are things that we have to do together, otherwise we remain just friends.'

'Good.' He spoke in a very different voice, as if relieved that something difficult was now over.

Jane felt easier, too. But there was also a feeling of something slipping away, of issues evaded when they should have been faced. It suddenly struck her that she also had feelings but no one had considered them. That meant she hadn't considered them herself! What her feelings were for Cal, she wasn't sure. Still, it was too late now.

'That call was from Social Services, a lady wanting to know what's happening to Helen,' Cal said. 'In fact, I know Margaret Claire quite well, we've co-operated on a few cases in the past. She's a friend, I suppose, but she won't let friendship get in the way of what she sees as her professional duties. She's been here to inspect where Helen is living, to assess the quality of care and write a report on her future.' Cal frowned. 'As you know, there's quite a bit of money that will ultimately be Helen's. That complicates things. If there's money involved then Social Services are always very wary.'

'So they should be,' said Jane. 'We've got nothing to hide, have we?'

'Perhaps not. When I first talked to Margaret I indicated that I wished—I expected—to adopt Helen and that no one else would be interested. She's a little perturbed that you have turned up.'

'Well, I don't intend to disappear again. Don't worry, Cal, if we support each other I'm sure things will be fine.'

'I'm sure, too. She's coming to see us in a couple of days, she says she'll give us time to settle down. I'd like it if we could tell her that—'

There was a phone extension in the kitchen, and now it rang.

'Not again! That phone will be the death of me,' he snarled, but he still rose to answer it.

Jane made for the door, 'One last thing,' she said, 'and then we'll never mention it again.'

'And that is?'

She wasn't quite sure why she said it. Perhaps it was the sense of mischief that had got her into so much trouble in the past. 'I really enjoyed being kissed by you.'

He looked at her balefully but said nothing.

When Lyn brought Helen back to the house later, Jane was touched to see the eagerness with which Cal opened his arms, and the speed with which Helen ran to him. The four of them sat round the kitchen table and Helen told them how she had spent her day. But Jane was thoroughly jet-lagged and Cal was in much the same state. After a while Lyn said, quite sympathetically, 'You two look exhausted. Why don't you go and get some sleep? I'll put Helen to bed and let myself out.'

Cal looked at Jane. 'I've missed my little girl but it seems like a good idea. What about you, Jane?'

Jane stood, leaned over to kiss Helen. 'See you in the morning, sweetheart,' she said. 'Auntie Jane and Uncle Cal are so tired they have to go to bed now.'

'You'll be here in the morning?' Helen's voice was wary.

Cal answered. 'We'll both be here Helen.' Then he and Jane left.

*　*　*

Next morning Jane rose late. When she hurried down to the kitchen Cal and Helen were finishing breakfast. Cal spooned the last few cornflakes into Helen's mouth then waved the spoon vaguely at the table. 'Breakfast is do-it-yourself,' he said. 'Tea, coffee, toast, cereals. I'm going to work now. Lyn will be here in a quarter of an hour. I thought that for the next few days the three of us could share looking after Helen. Until we get things sorted.'

'Seems like a good idea.' Jane was realising that she just couldn't demand to look after her niece. There were a lot of decisions to be made first.

Cal took a facecloth from the sink and, with much noisy but insincere protesting from Helen, wiped her face. Then he kissed her. 'Have a good day and we'll draw more pictures later.' Then he was gone.

'Uncle Cal is a good drawer,' Helen said placidly. 'Is there more orange juice?'

'I'll pour you some, sweetheart,' Jane said. She wanted to be part of this happy domestic scene. She was thinking how contented Cal had been with Helen—more contented than she had ever seen him. For a while the hard man had disappeared.

Lyn arrived shortly afterwards and the three of them were thinking about going for a walk when the phone rang. It was Cal, from the surgery. First he checked that Lyn had arrived and then said, 'I need a favour. We're very busy here, Jane, so would you like to lend me a hand for half an hour? I've got a patient and I really need a nurse to help me see to her. It ought to be done at once and it so happens there just isn't a nurse available.'

'Pleased to help,' Jane said. 'I'll be round in two minutes.'

She walked round to the surgery entrance and was met

by Eunice Padgett, the practice manager. Eunice was a large, middle-aged lady who seemed to spread calm wherever she went.

'Welcome to the team, Jane,' she said. 'Here's a white coat and you're in the first room on the left. Don't let him bully you.'

'Not a chance,' said Jane. But she was a little nervous as she knocked on Cal's door. This was the first time he had seen her in her professional capacity.

'Ah, Nurse Hall,' Cal said smoothly, 'this is Andrea Cannock. Could you help her undress and lie on the couch, please? We need to check a couple of things. Andrea has just had a fall onto the corner of a stool and has badly bruised her lower abdomen.'

Jane realised at once why he had sent for her. Andrea was young, frightened, in pain, possibly even a bit hysterical. It would have been a foolish male doctor who gave her an intimate examination without a chaperone.

Andrea wasn't a good patient. She wriggled, tensed, jerked on the couch and complained of pain when there couldn't be any. Eventually Jane held both her hands, somehow made her talk about how there was nothing, really nothing for a young girl to do in Keldale. And then there was the snapping sound as Cal pulled off his gloves and he said, 'Well, that's fine, Andrea. You can get dressed now. And what I'd like you to do is...'

'You were good,' he said to Jane five minutes later, when Andrea had gone. 'You kept that girl wonderfully calm. I might even offer you a job.'

'I might even accept,' she said. And she wondered why he looked at her so thoughtfully. Did he want her to work for him? She thought that perhaps it would be a good idea.

When she went back to Helen and Lyn, things were

hard. The little girl was weeping, asking where her parents were. A dozen times Jane tried the techniques taught her by a bereavement counsellor. Perhaps they helped Helen a little but by the end of the morning Jane felt emotionally drained.

'I've just got to be tougher,' she said to Lyn.

'You look all in,' Lyn said honestly. 'Why don't I take Helen out for a walk, then go back to my place? I can cope now, I think the worst is over. You can come over later this afternoon.'

Jane pondered a minute. 'All right,' she said. 'But I'll be there.'

She was sitting in Cal's kitchen, her shoulders slumped, when he came in. 'I thought you were working!' she said hastily.

'I am. I just called round for a couple of papers I need. Where's Helen?'

'Round at Lyn's house.'

Cal looked at her closely. She tried to appear bright and cheerful but it was an effort.

'You've had a bad morning.' It was a statement rather than a question.

'Not really. I'm still a bit tired, I suppose, and I...' She realised it was no good trying to deceive him. 'Yes, I've had a bad morning. Helen wants to know where her parents are. So do I for that matter.'

He came round the table, rested an arm on her shoulder. 'We all think of Helen first,' he said. 'That is fair, it is fine. But there are others who suffer just as much. You do and I do. I wonder what would have happened between us if there hadn't been Helen to worry about.'

This was something she had never thought of. 'Just us two? Would you still have come out to America to tell me?'

'Yes I would have. And, Jane…being with you the past few days has really helped me.'

This both surprised and pleased her. 'It has? Cal, that's a lovely thing to say.'

'Well, we have some things in common,' he said gruffly. 'Now, what are you going to do this afternoon? We appear to be sticking to the old programme, where Lyn has Helen at her house for a lot of the time. But her home is here.'

Jane had noticed that he would never talk for long about his own feelings, even admit to having them. It was a pity, really.

'I'm almost out of clothes and there's a limit to the time I can live out of my rucksack. Did you say that you have the keys to…to Marie's house?'

'Yes, I have the keys. Do you feel up to going there? It's going to be a strain on you.'

'It's something I've got to do. And the longer I put it off, the harder it will be.'

'Well, would you like me to come with you? I have some time this afternoon.'

It was very tempting. But she knew she had to resist. 'It's good of you to offer, but I think that it's something that I ought to do on my own. It'll help me to face up to things.'

He brooded for a moment. 'You could be right. But don't forget you've taken a battering in the past few days. You're not invulnerable.'

'I certainly don't feel it,' she assured him. 'I know my weaknesses. But I really ought to go there.'

'You know in time we'll have to go through the entire house? Decide what to get rid of, what to sell, what to store.'

'I know. The thought appals me. But we'll do it together.'

'We'll do it together,' he agreed. 'Jane…I like doing things with you. In some ways we make a good team.'

'A team! Not a partnership or…?'

'Being a team will do for now,' he said firmly. 'Let the future take care of itself. Now, I'll fetch the keys. Sure you'll be OK?'

'I'll be fine,' she said.

When he'd gone Jane wondered about what he had said. Just a team for now. But he saw them having some kind of future. With an odd thrill she realised she was quite curious about their future.

Yesterday's grey skies had gone, today was glorious. Overhead was a deep blue sky, set in a bowl of green hills. Jane walked through the village and felt happy to be alive.

This was where she had been born and grown up. She said hello to a couple of people she'd known for years. Some of the buildings had changed use, been added to, a couple even knocked down. But in general the village hadn't changed. And as she walked she felt a sense of contentment, of home-coming. Why had she ever wanted to go away?

But as she neared her sister's house, the feeling of elation disappeared. She'd had so many happy times here in her short stays over the past four years. Those times would never come back.

The house was in a small estate on the outskirts of the village, designed to fit in with the older buildings. The walls were of grey stone, the roof of slate. Jane had always liked it.

She fitted the key in the door, and hesitated. Out here

the sun was bright. She could go for a walk and her gloomy thoughts might disappear. No. Some things just had to be faced.

The house was silent. Even though it had only been empty for a few days, it felt unused. She forced herself to walk through all the rooms on the ground floor, to cope with the memories each room brought back. Finally she entered the kitchen. There was her sister's portable radio on a shelf, and Jane remembered how when Marie was doing her housework she would carry it from room to room. Jane reached for it, clicked on a music programme, tucked it under her arm. The music made things just a bit easier to bear.

She went upstairs, intending to go straight to her own little room, to the cupboard where her clothes and belongings were kept. But she had started something she knew she had to finish.

Her sister's bedroom. The double bed, still made, the fitted wardrobes down one side. Jane opened a door, saw her sister's serried clothes. There was a new evening dress, a long blue silk dress, still in its plastic cover. It had never been worn. Marie had written to her about it, said she was going to a summer ball in it. Jane sighed. How many of her own plans had never come true?

She lay on her sister's bed, remembering, capturing odd moments. Marie had been quite different from her, perhaps that was why the two used to get on so well. Marie had been the home-maker, only ever wanting her own husband, house and family. She had been a legal secretary and Peter a solicitor in nearby Kendal. All three of them had been local and had gone to the same school, had known each other for years. Cal had been older and Jane had never met him before the wedding. He'd spent most of his adult life training in London. Jane thought of the long, blue, unworn dress. No use moping. She walked briskly to her own room, opened her cupboard. She took the radio with her.

First of all she needed clothes. She piled things onto the bed and went to find a suitcase. It would be nice to show Cal that on occasion she could dress quite smartly. Not that she had many dresses.

Why should she think of Cal? As she packed she thought of him, remembered the kiss the day before. She had put it out of her mind for a while, but now she could think. As he had said, they had both been tired, jet-lagged, upset. Still, that kiss had been something. It had stirred feelings in her that she couldn't recollect experiencing before.

And what about that other kiss, the one at the wedding, when she'd been so curt with him? Why should she have cared that he was still—just—married?

In one of her frequent letters to Marie, she'd asked—apparently casually—about Cal's wedding. Marie had written back and told her that the two of them—she and Peter—had gone to London for Cal's wedding. It had been a very small affair, a registry office ceremony and then lunch at a nearby restaurant. The bride had been beautiful, but standoffish. The marriage had lasted barely six months, there had been lots of ill feeling and a messy divorce. Peter had offered to act for his brother as solicitor, but the offer had been declined. Peter had worried about Cal, but Cal had said nothing to anyone, had lost himself in work. He'd always been able to do that. Then, just before Marie's wedding, Cal had taken the post in Keldale. All this had happened, of course, while Jane had been abroad.

Jane wondered what kind of woman could marry Cal

and then lose him after six months. What did she look like? Suddenly, she had an idea.

Carrying the radio with her, she ran downstairs. Marie had been a great collector of photographs. Under the television was a line of albums, two for each year. Jane saw the silver one that held the wedding photographs and quickly looked away.

It was easy to work out the year when Cal's wedding had been. With the radio playing beside her, Jane quickly leafed through the relevant album. There were other things she remembered—herself with a new rucksack, setting off for Peru, an office party with Marie and Peter. And here was a section on Cal and Fiona's wedding. Fiona?

There were just two pages of pictures, obviously all taken by Marie herself. No official photographs. The bride and groom wore ordinary clothes, no morning suit or long trailing dress. And only a handful of friends around them.

She peered at Cal's picture, feeling an odd anger that she couldn't explain. This had been years ago when he'd been a much younger man, gazing adoringly at his new wife. His face looked different—less harsh, less careworn. What had happened to him since?

Then Jane looked at the new wife. Even with her inexperienced eye she could tell that the dress, although not a wedding one, was expensive. The woman was undoubtedly very attractive. But Jane knew at once the description that would suit her. She was a glacial blonde. She had a small smile, seemed happy enough. Not the woman for Cal, though. Definitely not the woman for Cal. Cal needed someone who...

'Fascinated?'

Jane shrieked, and the album tumbled from her hands.

She had thought she was alone. The radio had hidden any noise and… She turned and there behind her was Cal. He looked even more intimidating than ever.

'You gave me a shock, you shouldn't do that!'

'The door was open and I did knock. But the music was playing and you were engrossed. Why the fascination with my ex-wife?'

Jane flushed. 'I wasn't looking at your ex-wife. I know that Marie kept her albums here and I wanted to skim through and…'

Why should she bother? He was looking at her with disbelief. 'All right, I was vaguely curious about her.' He looked at her again. 'All right, all right, I was plain nosy. I wondered what kind of woman could make you, could make you…'

He picked up the album, looked at it thoughtfully. 'This is the first I've ever seen of these,' he said. 'I've got rid of all the pictures I had of her. It's hard to believe that I was that grinning idiot.'

'You look happy,' Jane said. 'And your new wife looks beautiful and…and…' She stared at the little picture. What was the expression on Fiona's face?

'Self-satisfied?' Cal suggested.

And that was just it. The expression was self-satisfied. Those blank, beautiful eyes were those of a cat who had been at the cream.

'I'm sorry if it disturbed you, my looking at the pictures,' she said. 'It's none of my business and, Lord knows, you've got enough to worry about right now. I know you feel bad about her. Do you ever hear from her?'

Her took the album from her, stared at the pictures for a couple of minutes, then shut the book with a bang.

'I never hear from her and I never want to. That episode of my past is finished, done with. Now you and I have to concentrate on the future, not the past. For Helen's sake.'

'The past makes the future,' Jane said quietly. 'Helen is just old enough to remember her parents. We want her to have a new life, a happy life, but she should never forget the love they had for her.'

'I agree with you,' he said. 'We may disagree on the right way to find her a happy life, but I'm glad we agree in principle.'

He went to sit in an easy chair and gazed down at her. After a moment she moved to sit in an easy chair opposite him.

'You say that the past makes the future,' he said after a while. 'D'you think I've been made like I am by being married and divorced?'

Jane was apprehensive. She wanted to learn more about him, she was vastly curious. But she wasn't sure how to approach him. 'I would have thought being married affected you,' she said cautiously. 'You don't seem to have a high opinion of it. Or of women in general. Are you going to tell me why?'

'Tell you all my secrets? Why should I?'

'Because I suspect that you've never confided in anyone,' she said boldly. 'Marie said in her letters that Peter didn't know what had gone wrong. Don't you know that confession is good for the soul?'

He looked surprised. 'You're a lot more shrewd than you appear at first,' he said, 'and you're pushy, too.'

'I have had complaints,' she admitted.

'All right,' he said. 'I'm still not sure why, but I'll tell you.'

Cal frowned, as if trying to set the story straight in his mind. 'I was a junior registrar in a big hospital in

London, doing well and enjoying my work. But I knew that ultimately I wanted to come back here to the Lake District to be a GP. I met Fiona. She was doing something important in the hospital, something to do with finance, but she didn't really need to work. She came from a rich family. We got on well, I thought I had fallen in love.' He paused, looked at her broodingly.

'Perhaps you were in love,' Jane said. 'Why blame yourself?'

'Why indeed? Anyway, Fiona wanted to get married at once. I was working like a lunatic and I thought it would be fairer to her if we waited. She said it wasn't fair to her to make her wait. And all the time she knew that my ultimate aim was to move back up here to the north.

'Anyway, we got married. Things weren't too bad, she had a lot of family around and she managed to amuse herself while I was at work. Then I was offered a job in Chicago. I must say it was a great opportunity. An enormous salary, high lifestyle and an apartment overlooking the Lake. She was very keen for me to take it. But I said, no, we had agreed that in time I would look for a partnership in the Lake District. And we had the first of our really serious rows.'

'Are you sure that you made it clear to her that you intended to come back up here? Sure you didn't make your mind up afterwards?'

He frowned. 'That's what she said. But I remembered very clearly. We'd talked about it and she'd agreed. She thought that after we were married she'd be able to change my mind.'

'Some chance,' Jane muttered.

He looked at her disapprovingly, but said nothing about her comment. 'Anyway, the next thing was that she announced she was pregnant. It shouldn't have happened. She said it was an accident but I suspect she did it on purpose. But though it was unplanned, I was really looking forward to being a father. Then she said that we had to go to Chicago, we needed the money to support our lifestyle. No way was she going to bring up a child in the nasty little hospital flat that we had.'

He paused a moment, smiled. 'Actually, I quite liked the flat. But the rows got worse.'

'Some women are affected that way by pregnancy,' Jane suggested. 'It's not always fair to judge a woman at that time. Her hormones are in a mess.'

'I'm a doctor! I know all about pregnancy and women's hormones!'

'I'm sure you do. Carry on with what you were saying.' Jane was fascinated.

'As I said, the rows got worse. Every night, in fact. I even thought of going to Chicago, but I certainly didn't want to. But then there was the chance of a partnership up here, and this was exactly what I had always wanted. I told her, and the rows got worse. One row went on all night. I was working too hard and I was dead beat—not only lack of sleep but emotion itself is wearying. Anyway, I made a mistake. Never mind what drug it was, I prescribed a hundred mil instead of ten. The nurse spotted it, for which I will always be grateful, because otherwise the patient would have died.'

Jane could tell that the memory still had power to horrify him. 'These things happen,' she said softly. 'Anyone can make a mistake.'

'Doctors shouldn't. At least they shouldn't let their private life get in the way of their profession. Whether it was my fault or my wife's fault I didn't know. But it wasn't going to happen again. So I went home to tell her that. And I found her packing. She said I was selfish, thought only of myself and not her. I said what about the baby? There was no baby, it was only three months, she'd had a termination.'

'She'd had a what?' Jane was horrified.

'Having a baby just wasn't convenient for her. She didn't want to stay with me and she was not going to be a single mother either. So within six months we'd moved from passion, deep love, to hatred.'

'What happened to her?'

He shrugged. 'She married a rich doctor, a plastic surgeon, and the last I heard they were living in New York and were blissfully happy.' He smiled bleakly. 'Life was good to her after me. Anyway, I decided then that I wasn't going to trust women with my feelings. I've been very happy since.'

Jane considered this story. 'Not all women are like that, you know,' she said.

'Possibly not. But why risk it?'

'Why indeed?' Jane just didn't know what to say next. Cal himself now seemed content to say nothing, to sit there as if his story—his confession almost—had tired him. But Jane's thoughts were racing. And suddenly she realised something.

'You told me that story for a reason, didn't you?' she asked.

'You were curious. You wanted to know.'

'True. But why tell me? I bet you've not told many people—if you've told any.'

He didn't reply at first. When he did speak his voice had changed and was measured, authoritarian. 'I'm determined that Helen should have a better life than my little…than my possible unborn child would have had. I want to bring her up, provide certainty, give her the happy upbringing that I had. I want to adopt her. I'm very pleased that you should be a favourite auntie, I know you'll be good at it. There'll always be a place for you to stay. But in a few months you'll be off, you can't help it. And Helen will be upset.'

'I'm me, Jane Hall! I'm not your ex-wife!'

'I know that. But the fact remains, your lifestyle over the past few years hasn't been the ideal one for bringing up a young child.'

'I could change!'

'Now, where have I heard that before?' he mused.

There seemed to be nothing else she could say.

He went on, 'Incidentally, Margaret Claire, the Social Services woman, is coming to see me at six tonight. And while she's here I want to tell her formally that I wish to adopt Helen.'

'Well, I need to meet her, too. I want to make sure I'm involved in Helen's life, too.'

Now his face was hard. 'Well, I'm certain that I don't want Helen thinking of you as a mother who is absent most of the time. I'll bring her up, with help from Miriam. You can love her—but from a distance.'

This just wasn't fair! Jane tried hard to control her temper, but it was no good. She had to say what she felt. 'I can see why your wife left you. You're incapable of seeing any point of view but your own. Now, listen! Helen is as much my responsibility as yours and I'm going to play my part. Not because of duty, or because I ought to, but because I love her and I want to. We'll co-operate in bringing her up. If we don't, then we fight. But one thing is certain. I won't just lie down, roll over and do as you say!'

CHAPTER FOUR

JANE was upstairs, finishing her packing, Cal sat alone.
He had spent so many happy hours in this room, he remembered. Marie and Peter had been so much, so obviously in love, it had been heart-warming just to be with
them. He had almost envied them their happiness.

Why couldn't he have found a woman he could love
as Peter had loved Marie?

Which question brought him to Jane. Jane wasn't like
Marie. Where Marie had been calming, Jane was argu-
mentative. Where Marie had been willing to be guided,
Jane was determined to have her own way.

He thought he could quite…like Jane. He did like her.
If only she didn't manage to annoy him so much.

They parted very coolly. He insisted on driving her back
to his house with the two cases she had packed. Then he
went on his afternoon calls and she went to Lyn's house
to pick up Helen. For the first time she was going to be
with Helen on her own. Lyn had told her she wanted to
drive into Kendal.

Helen had the resilience of a child, the morning's misery forgotten. She played happily with Jane in Cal's
kitchen, drawing on large sheets of paper, dressing and
undressing her dolls. Jane was enjoying herself.

As she played, a part of her mind considered and re-
considered what Cal had told her. There were two things
she was certain of. First, she felt a great sympathy for
the man. Second, there was no way she was going to

hand over Helen to him. They would have to bring her up together. But how? She couldn't imagine how the situation would resolve itself and her mind reeled as she considered option after option, and rejected them all.

Lyn called in later with a dress she had bought for Helen. Jane made tea and they had a long amiable gossip, talking of people Jane remembered and the newcomers to the village. Helen played happily in a corner of the kitchen.

Quite by accident Jane mentioned that she had met Cal, and that they had had an argument. 'He doesn't want me to have a half-share in Helen's future, Lyn. He thinks I'm a fly-by-night.' Then she considered. 'I suppose I am, really. But I want to change.'

'He's a very good boss and doctor,' Lyn said. 'Please, don't quote me, but perhaps like many doctors he's got a tendency to think that he always knows what's right. And often he is right. This practice used to be amiable but a bit inefficient. Now it's happy and efficient. There's a staff of over twenty-five, and we all think Cal is wonderful.'

'Must be great to be so popular,' Jane muttered.

'Of course, there are lots of staff changes. The trainee doctors—the registrars that is—they stay one year at the most. Other staff come and go. Remember Enid Sharpe?'

'Nurse Sharpe! I remember her giving me an injection when I was a child. She said it wouldn't hurt. I didn't believe her but she was right.'

'She's still the district nurse. But she's fifty-five now, a grandmother of three already and thinking about retirement. She told Cal that she wouldn't mind going part-time, work-sharing for the next five years. But he's not to worry too much about it.'

'So they're looking for someone who could work as a part-time district nurse,' Jane said slowly.

'Sort of. If they come across someone suitable. And if they did find someone, they could move into the cottage next door to me. It's vacant, you know.'

Jane gazed into Lyn's brown eyes, but the midwife's expression gave nothing away. 'Are you telling me this for a reason?' she asked.

'No, not at all. It's just gossip I thought you'd be interested.'

'Oh, I'm interested all right. I'm interested that Cal hasn't mentioned it himself.'

Jane and Cal were due to meet Margaret Claire, the social worker, at six o'clock. They had to present a united front. Nothing could be worse than the two closest relatives not being able to agree on Helen's future. Lyn left and Cal came into the kitchen an hour early to try to sort things out. He wasn't in a good mood.

'I hope you aren't going to upset things just because they don't fit in with your ideas,' he said, his face stern. 'That would be selfish in the extreme.'

Jane decided she could swallow this insult—but only this one. 'I've got an idea,' she said. 'Something that we could both agree on. Firstly, I want to say that I think that you would be a wonderful father. In some ways if not in all.'

This raised a little smile. 'I shan't ask where I fall down. I suspect that telling me would take too long. But thanks for the compliment. I do value it.'

'Good. Now, I think we need a period of calm. Not only Helen, but you and me. None of us should take any long-term decisions.' She paused a moment—this was the difficult bit. 'I gather you're looking for a part-time district nurse?'

'Who told you that?' His voice was sharp.

'It's common knowledge,' she said hurriedly. 'Lots of people in the practice know. I am qualified, I can provide references, I think I could do the job. For the next six months I'd like to share looking after Helen with you, and work part-time as your district nurse. At the end of that time we'll review the situation. If, as you think, I've got itchy feet, then off I go. If we're working well together, then we'll reconsider everything.'

Jane had no idea what he was thinking as his face was blank. He said, 'Give me a minute, I need to consider this.'

Well, that was a start. He wasn't rejecting her plan out of hand.

Eventually, he said, 'I'll have to consult my partners and the district nurse herself. What's good for me might not be good for the practice. But I like the idea very much. And when Margaret arrives, we can provide a united front.'

He smiled, perhaps rather reluctantly. 'What will I do if Helen grows up as manipulative and as determined as you? Life will be hell!'

'Only partly. She'll also be your little girl, lovely and exasperating, and life will be heaven. Well, some bits of it will be.'

'What a prospect! I can't wait.'

Jane liked Margaret Claire at once. She was about forty, with a cap of blonde hair, and managed to seem efficient and compassionate at the same time. She looked at Jane with frank interest.

'I'm very pleased to meet you. I gather you're a bit of

a wanderer as Cal had to fly to America to find you. Will you be off again soon?'

'No. I have responsibilities here—more than that, I want to stay. I'll be here for at least six months, and in all probability permanently. I'm hoping that Cal and I can work together to provide a loving home for Helen.'

'That sounds good. I like the idea of six months—it's not a good idea for anyone to rush into decisions quickly. Cal?'

'Jane and I can sort things out in time. The six months will give us a breathing space.'

Margaret opened her bag, rustled through some papers. 'Well, I've made a domiciliary visit here and you know I've been very pleased with Helen being looked after by Lyn Pierce as well. If circumstances change radically though, I shall need to come and visit again. You'll let me know?'

'Naturally,' Cal said. 'We need your advice. When do you have to make a full report to your bosses?'

Margaret sighed. 'It's going to be complicated. Have you got any more for me on the legal situation?'

'Helen will be...financially very well off,' Cal said flatly. 'She's the only heir, and there's the house, insurance policies, other money to come in. I've told you Peter was a solicitor. The senior partner of his firm will be handling the money angle and I've asked her to get in touch with you direct.'

Margaret nodded gloomily. 'Just what we need. We all have to step very carefully. If there's big money involved, the courts will be extra-careful. There's been a few nasty cases here and there.'

Jane felt she had to interrupt. 'What's the problem? Helen has family who love her, who want to look after her, to care for her. Isn't that good enough?'

Margaret looked grim. 'We have to be careful but I'm
sure that ultimately there will be no problem. Not every
family is as loving as I'm sure this one will be. But I'll
fill in an interim report, keep dropping in and we'll get
things sorted out in time. Miss Hall, I'm very glad to
have met you but could I have a word with Cal alone?'

'If it's about Helen then I want to hear it,' Jane said,
instantly on the defensive.

'I wouldn't dream of leaving you out of any conversation about Helen,' Margaret said. 'It's just that I've got
a problem with one of Cal's patients, a teenage girl. It's
all quite proper, we have consent to talk about her and
so on, but it is, of course, confidential.'

'Of course,' said Jane. 'Sorry if I seemed a bit…well,
over-anxious.'

'I understand.' Margaret's smile was sympathetic.

Jane bathed Helen and put her to bed that evening. It was
a job she loved. Helen was a little water baby. She liked
lots of water, she liked foam, she liked the four yellow
ducks Jane had bought her. The two of them were having
a wonderful time playing when a male voice behind them
asked, 'Room in here for another one?' It was Cal's
voice.

Jane felt a tiny surge of pleasure. 'Come and join the
soap brigade.'

He had changed from his more formal medical gear
into the usual T-shirt and chinos, and looked good in
them. 'I decided that evening surgery could do without
me,' he said cheerfully. 'I wanted to come and say goodnight to my niece.' He leaned over and kissed the top of
a wet head. 'How are you, honey?'

'Uncle Cal! These are my new ducks. This one is
Betty, this one is Bobby, this one is…is…'

'Bertie,' Jane supplied. 'And the last is?'

'This one is Bunny! I've got foam all over me, Uncle Cal.'

'You're a lovely foamy little girl,' said Cal, and leaned over the bath to froth up the water.

'You'll get your shirt wet,' Jane said, who was dressed in a borrowed pinafore.

'Doesn't matter.' He was stirring up more bubbles, to squeals of delight. 'How are you taking to child management?'

'I have had experience before,' she pointed out. 'In Peru I worked in an orphanage. I fed, bathed and treated eight little girls as well as doing my nursing duties for a year.'

He looked at her seriously. 'I didn't know that. I'm really impressed.' He pushed a yellow duck into a great ball of foam. 'I've been thinking about your idea of working part-time as my district nurse. How would you like to—? You want to get out now, darling? OK, rinse time and then teeth.'

She watched him lean over the bath, rinse Helen and then wrap her in a towel. He lifted her to the washbasin and set her on a stool, and the two cleaned her teeth together. Then he carried her downstairs, put on her pyjamas and held her between his knees as he dried and brushed her hair. It was a simple domestic scene and it made Jane see Cal in a totally different light. He looked contented. He was a wonderful uncle—would be a wonderful father. The man who could be harsh, stern, had totally disappeared.

He sat Helen on his knee and winked at Jane. 'What story do you want tonight?'

'Last night I read about the blue bunnies. I want it again.'

Wordlessly Jane offered him the book.

He took it and began, 'Once upon a time…'

Jane watched as he read the story, and saw the little eyes flicker and close. 'I'll take her to bed,' she murmured.

'In a minute. There's no hurry, let her lie here for a while.' So the three sat in silence. Jane found it strangely peaceful sitting there, watching Cal. He was cradling the little girl, obviously with love. After a while he looked up and caught her watching him.

She flushed. 'I've been a bit selfish,' she said. 'All I've been able to think about is that I've lost a sister. But you've lost a brother. Does it…does it hurt you like it hurts me? You never seem to show much emotion.'

'It hurts,' he said. 'Peter and I were very different and we spent a lot of time apart. But recently I've been seeing…that is, I saw…a lot of him. We were growing together more. And I was very fond of Marie, too.'

He must have seen the pain in Jane's eyes as his voice instantly became impersonal, professional. 'She's fast asleep now. Do you want to put her to bed?'

Wordlessly, Jane took the little bundle from him and went upstairs.

When she came back Cal seemed determined to remain businesslike, as if he wanted to hide the little glimpse she'd had of his softer side. 'As I said, I've been thinking about your idea of working for me part-time. I phoned Enid and she's quite interested in the idea. Would you like to go out with her tomorrow morning?'

'I'd love to. Are you offering me a job?'

'No. I'm interviewing you. Or, to be more exact, Enid will interview you.' He grinned. 'I should tell you that the unofficial interview you get from her will be the all-important one. Enid won't hand over until she's entirely satisfied with any replacement.'

'Any test, any examination.' Jane smiled. 'I can only do my best.'

'I suspect that will be more than enough.' He pondered. 'Enid's time is divided between house calls and a little work in the surgery. I think a good idea would be if eventually somone could take over most of her distant home visits. She's got a touch of arthritis, she's not as mobile as she used to be.'

'I'll do anything, but that would suit me fine.'

'Good. I'll get you an application form to fill in and I'll want a full CV. We'll need to see what you've been doing over the past few years. There'll be no end of red tape, but I think you should be an asset to the practice. And if we offer you a post, Eunice will arrange an induction programme.'

All this made Jane feel good. Cal was treating her as a fellow professional, and she liked it. 'You're thinking of the job, not of Helen, aren't you?' she said.

He looked surprised. 'Of course I am! No way would I let personal considerations affect my professional work.' Then he grinned again. 'But I must say, it would make my life very much simpler. Now, Enid will pick you up at the surgery at half past eight tomorrow. Eunice has found you a uniform, it'll be in the kitchen waiting for you this evening. Lyn will help out with Helen for a few more days and will come round here whenever she's needed.'

He stood. 'You're babysitting now. I'm afraid there's work I've got to do in the surgery.'

Shyly, Jane asked, 'You haven't time to stay a while? I could make us some tea.'

She saw him hesitate. But then his jaw firmed, his

eyes avoided hers. 'I'd better go,' he said. 'There's a lot I still have to do. Perhaps…later.'

When Cal had gone Jane felt restless. She wasn't quite certain what she wanted out of life, what her next move was to be. Coming back home was a big change. How would she cope with being a surrogate mother to Helen? How would she cope with Cal?

He intrigued her. He was a mixture, half arrogant, half accommodating. No one could be a better uncle to Helen than he. But he was suspicious of her and, Jane supposed, of most women. His ex-wife had done a good job on him. If they were to work together, they would both have to learn to give way a little. Jane knew she would find it hard, and she suspected Cal would find it even harder.

For a moment she thought about the job she might take. The practice covered a wide area. It was based in Keldale, which was quite a large village, but there were a dozen smaller villages and no end of farms. Over in the west she could see the peaks of the Langdales. The mountains were much lower than those she was used to in America, but she knew that they could be just as dangerous. Cal had told her that he was on the list of call-out doctors for Mountain Rescue. She pondered. If she stayed, perhaps she could volunteer to be one of the call-out nurses. If she stayed.

She, Cal and Helen had a lightning breakfast next morning, then Lyn arrived and Jane hurried next door to wait in the surgery for Enid to collect her. It felt good to be in a uniform again—she hadn't worn one for quite some time. She remembered Enid at once, though she hadn't seen her in nearly ten years. Her figure was still spare and erect, her hair was still pulled tight in a bun, though there were now grey streaks in the black.

'Jane Hall,' Enid said. 'Family used to live at the top of Cryers' Lane. You didn't cry when you broke your arm.'

'That was nearly twenty years ago!'

'Well, I haven't forgotten. You were very brave.'

Jane decided that she was off to a good start with Enid. But she would have to remember—the older nurse had a good memory. She probably wouldn't forget any carelessness either.

It had been agreed that Jane would just observe on this first session. She could get to know the routes, meet some of the people involved. First they had to do half an hour's paperwork at the surgery, look up referrals and collect any drugs or dressings they might need. Then they set off in Enid's four-wheel-drive vehicle. Jane had noticed that all the partners and nurses had these. In winter they would often be very necessary.

The first call was to check up on a small boy who had broken his leg. Enid wanted to be sure that he wasn't fretting too much or having difficulty with the plaster, which ran right up to his thigh. No problem there. His mother had organised a rota of friends and family to keep young Richard amused.

After that they called on Mr and Mrs Grantham. Mr Grantham had just had an operation for a cataract in his left eye. Mrs Grantham assured them that he was doing fine. It took quite an effort from Enid to get an answer from Mr Grantham, but he, too, thought that he was doing fine.

So far the driving had been easy. But now Enid turned off the main road onto a secondary road, and then from that onto a rough track that seemed to lead straight upwards. They bounced and jerked, and Jane saw the little grimace of pain on Enid's face. This wasn't good for her arthritis. But she didn't complain, and Jane decided not to ask her about it. Enid had her pride.

'If you think this is bad now, you should see it in winter,' Enid said. 'The stream runs onto this path—you can get axle deep in mud.'

'I can imagine. Who are we calling on now?'

'Jenny Lawson. She's on medication for depression, I try to drop in every week if I can. There's not a lot physiologically wrong with Jenny. She had two miscarriages and then two kids. She manages with them—but she just can't get out. Only one vehicle, and the husband needs it for work. He's a good man, but it's hard to scratch a living from this land.'

'So she's more or less imprisoned,' Jane said. 'That's not good. I can feel for her.'

Enid realised that Jane was a sympathetic audience. 'She lived in town before, lived there all her life. I don't think she realised what she was coming to.'

They bumped to a stop outside a whitewashed cottage. Jane looked round at derelict farming equipment, run-down barns. The place didn't look prosperous.

As they pulled up a woman came promptly to the cottage door, a baby in her arms. She smiled wearily, but her pleasure was obvious. 'Hello, Enid, nice of you to call. Kettle's on—do you want a cup of tea?'

Jane climbed out and walked round the back of the car. She saw the woman's stringy hair, slumped shoulders, defeated expression.

Enid said, 'I've brought a visitor, she might be joining the practice.'

The woman shifted the baby to her other arm and held

out her hand. 'My goodness! It's Jane, Jane Hall. How are you Jane? It's good to see you.'

Jane tried to smile back and hide her dismay. 'Jenny Wilson? Is it Jenny Wilson? My, you've…grown.' The word she had been going to use was 'changed'.

Jane sat in the living room, balancing two-year-old Jack on one knee and her cup of tea on the other, while Enid examined four-year-old Rebecca. Jenny had done her best with the threadbare furniture and few pictures. Now it was summer, the room wasn't too bad. But she guessed that in winter, the room would be bitterly cold. There was a stone floor and only a fireplace for heating.

'I had three good years after I left school,' Jenny was saying. 'I got a job in a clothes shop in Kendal and for two years I went to Benidorm in summer with my mates. Then I met Jerry, we fell in love and got married. And he brought me here.'

Jane remembered the vivacious girl two years behind her at school. So different from this weary creature! 'So everything is fine with Jerry?' she asked.

Jenny smiled. 'Of course it is. He loves me and he loves the kids. But he's out all day and I get lonely. It might be different when the kids have to go to school— though how we'll get them there I don't know.'

'I'm sure the council will arrange something,' Jane said. 'Then perhaps you could get a part-time job. Do you see many of your old friends at all?'

'No,' Jenny said simply. 'Will you call again? You could come with Enid—or you could call on your own.'

As they bounced down the path later Enid said, 'The right girl in the wrong place. Jenny needs to be with people, she just can't take loneliness. Some women can— some women like being on their own—but not Jenny.'

'There's nothing that can be done?' Jane asked.

'Not that I can think of. I call when I can. Her father's dead and her mother's not strong and doesn't drive. I've had a quiet word with the husband. He's trying to get a lease on a bigger farm somewhere nearer the main road. Then Jenny might see a few more people and she wouldn't need medication. Jerry's offered to give up farming, get a factory job or something—but Jenny won't let him. She knows he loves this life.'

Jane sighed. She knew that this was a problem that medicine couldn't solve.

The next two visits were quite straightforward. First there was a man who needed a weekly injection of antidepressant drugs. 'Would you like to do this one?' Enid asked carelessly.

Jane realised this was a test. 'If you want me to,' she said.

It wasn't too difficult—but she saw the alert way that Enid watched her. Fine, she liked people who were conscientious.

The second visit was a little more troublesome. Eighty-year-old Jim Benton was suffering from dermatitis.

'Started about four years ago,' Enid explained. 'Cal and I tried everything to find out what caused it. There was no obvious irritant—it wasn't light, it wasn't drugs, it wasn't plants.'

'Endogenous dermatitis,' Jane said. 'Usually found in older people and absolutely no precipitating factor found. I worked with a man in America who had it, he was rich and had spent a fortune looking for a cure. And he never found one.'

'I can imagine. However, Jim takes it quite well. He's

on steroids, but he copes. One of our better patients. We'll just call and have a look at his arms.'

Jim lived alone in a small house just off the main road. Both his house and garden were spotless. For thirty years Jim had been in the Royal Navy, and he told Jane that this had taught him the value of tidiness. 'Tidy home, tidy mind, tidy life,' he proclaimed. 'I learned that aboard.'

'I can see. Your garden is really lovely. Do you do much digging?'

'I don't need to. As I said, get things shipshape and they're easy to run.'

'I noticed,' Jane said gently, 'that you seemed to be a bit stiff when you stood up. You haven't been overdoing it in the garden, have you? Perhaps strained your back?'

'Just a bit of stiffness,' Jim said, waving a hand. 'Had it last week but it'll pass.'

But by now Enid was paying attention. She looked from Jane to Jim, and then said, 'Go on, Jane.'

Putting on what she always thought of as her po-face, Jane asked, 'Have you had any difficulty in passing water recently, Mr Benton?'

'Just a bit,' Jim muttered. 'Nothing to worry about, is there? It was worse in the convoys.'

Now it was Enid's turn. 'Any pains down below, Jim? You can talk to us, you know, we're both nurses.'

'It comes and goes. I don't want any fuss made, it's not important.'

'No blood in your urine?'

'Certainly not!'

But Enid took a glass phial out of her bag and handed it to Jim. 'Go and see if you can give me a specimen,' she said firmly. 'Not much, a couple of drops will do.'

When Jim returned Jane saw Enid dip a stick into the

specimen, look at it and frown. 'We'll get the doctor to come out and see you, Jim,' she said. 'He likes to keep in touch. It's possible that you've got a kidney stone.'

'Just a bit of backache!'

'There was blood in your urine, Jim. Not much, but enough. Now, if the pain gets much worse, then ring us.'

'Lot of fuss about nothing!'

A couple of minutes later they left. 'That was well spotted,' Enid said approvingly. 'I missed it. We'll get Cal to come out and see what he thinks.'

Jane felt she had passed some kind of test.

'So d'you like working the district?' Enid asked later as they drove home. 'Think you could do it day in, day out for years?'

'I like it. I know that it's summer now, and we're seeing things at their best. But I reckon I'd still like it if I was knee deep in mud or it was raining non-stop.'

'We'll see,' Enid said.

It was the sixth day of Jane's stay in Cal's house. She had been going out with Enid for three days, and already she, Cal and Helen seemed to have established a pattern of living together that suited them all. Either Cal or Jane got Helen out of bed while the other made a quick breakfast. Then they all ate together, sometimes watching cartoons on the small television. 'I used to sit and listen to Radio Four,' Cal told her. 'But I find this far more fun.' Then Lyn came round and they went out to work.

Jane had finished breakfast and was in her room. She was just about to go round to meet Enid when there was a knock on her door. Thinking that it was Lyn, she called, 'Come on.' But it was Cal.

He stepped inside and looked around. He hadn't been in her room since he'd first showed it to her. 'Quick message,' he said. 'Enid's going to be three quarters of an hour late, some kind of grandchild emergency. She didn't want you hanging round, waiting for her.'

'Nice of her to tell us,' Jane said. 'I'll play with Helen and Lyn for a bit.'

He didn't go at once but stood there looking rather uncertain. 'Are you comfortable here?'

'I can be comfortable anywhere. But this is a very pleasant room.'

'You've made it more than pleasant. You've made it your home.'

This compliment pleased her. All she had done had been to bring a few of her things from her sister's house. There were pictures and photographs, a few books, her throw on the bed. Nothing that wasn't portable, that couldn't be moved in five minutes. But it did make the room hers. 'It's my nest-building instinct,' she said, hoping he would see it as a joke.

But he didn't, he took her seriously. 'You do it everywhere you go? Try and make yourself a home from home?'

She'd never really thought about it, but what he'd said was true. 'I suppose I do. Wherever I am, there's always a couple of photographs to remind me of who I am, and what I've left behind.'

'What you've left behind? That's important to you?' He was quick.

'Very important. My roots are here.'

'I see. May I look round?'

She was pleased at his curiosity, that he wanted to know something of her past. 'Be my guest,' she said.

Cal scanned her books, took up a couple and glanced at them. 'Wainwright's walking guides?'

'I love his drawings. I could sit and look at them for ever.'

'Me, too. I have the complete set of books and a couple of his original drawings.'

'You have! Where? I've not seen them.'

'They're in a cupboard somewhere.'

Then he looked at the photographs. 'Where's this?' he asked. It was a picture of Jane surrounded by a group of giggling children. Behind her was a great mountain peak.

'That's the orphanage and school I told you about where I worked in Peru. I write to the kids once a month and I get a joint letter back. It helps their English, you know.'

'I see.' He seemed fascinated by the photograph.

'You're looking at the mountain?' she asked. 'It's beautiful, isn't it?'

'No I wasn't looking at the mountain. I was looking at you.'

Jane decided to change the subject. There was something she had been thinking about, something she hadn't yet brought up again. 'You know, Cal, I said before that this is a lovely house you have. But there's no impression of your taste, your feelings. I can't tell what you like. You have two Wainwright prints and they're in a cupboard. That's terrible! The only places that are home-like here are your study, the kitchen and Helen's bedroom.'

His voice was sardonic. 'You still think the place needs a woman's touch?'

'No. It needs your touch.'

He shrugged. 'I've had all that before. My ex-wife was always very keen on having a home that reflected her taste, that was a suitable background for her. It was only a tiny flat but it cost me a fortune in interior decorators. So now all I want is a place that's clean and comfortable.

That's all.' He sat on her bed and looked up at her. 'But, I must confess, this is pleasant. Do you want to advise me on how to make this place a home?'

She knew this was a joke. 'You don't need advice. Look at how well you've decorated Helen's room.'

'I did enjoy that. Mind you, Lyn gave me some advice. But I've left the rest until Miriam gets here.'

'Miriam! So you're going ahead with that plan, are you?'

'I have to do something, Jane.' His voice was calm, reasonable, as if what he was saying was completely obvious. 'The arrangement with Lyn is only temporary, she needs to start work soon.'

'But I thought that I...that we...'

'We have an agreement for six months and I will honour it! But at the end of that time you might decide to go. I won't make any decision about Helen without your consent, I told you that. But I must make sure that there's a permanent home somewhere for her. She needs to be settled. Margaret said so and I agree. Perhaps Miriam won't be needed as a substitute mother, in which case she can stay on as my housekeeper. I'm single. I'm doing well, I can afford her.'

Jane took a breath, told herself the best thing to do now was to remain calm and reasonable. Sound like he had sounded. But she just couldn't do it.

'I know...that is, I knew...Miriam Watts. She's intelligent, competent, manipulative. If you let her into this house you'll be married to her within a year.'

His laugh was harsh. 'That's a joke. One, I am not easy to manipulate. Two, I've been married. I'm very well aware that the disadvantages far outweigh the advantages. Now, let's talk about something else.'

CHAPTER FIVE

JANE knew she would never get over the horror of her sister's death. She would be working, playing with Helen, writing a letter, and suddenly the realisation would hit her again. Marie was dead. Then the tears would spring to her eyes as if she'd just heard the news for the first time.

But she was getting used to the situation. She spent a lot of time with Helen, that was therapy for her. And she knew that, in time, all grief passed.

Of all people, it was Enid who brought the subject up. Jane enjoyed working with her. Not only was she a very skilful district nurse, she also had the combination of compassion and realism that was so necessary. Some things just had to be accepted.

The two of them were driving out of Keldale early next morning when Enid said, 'Of course, I know the situation you're in. They say that work is the best cure for grief, but that's not entirely true. You've got to think, talk about the dead person. A lot of people say that the best thing to do is not to mention them. No, it isn't. Tell me about the last time you saw and talked to your sister.'

So Jane told her and although it was painful, at the end of her description, she felt a little better.

'Do you talk to Cal about your feelings?' Enid then demanded.

'No. Mostly we disagree over what Helen's future should be.'

'Might have guessed. Has he told you about his feelings, how sad he is?'

'No,' said Jane, after a moment's thought. 'I know he must be terribly upset—but he's never said so. Perhaps he was thinking of me.'

'He's a good doctor…but that man needs to learn how to let himself go, how to be vulnerable again. However, he's not who we're talking about. Have you been to your sister's grave yet?'

'No. Cal offered to take me, but I just couldn't face it. I want to go, but I just can't work up the courage.'

'In ten minutes we've got a call at a farm just the other side of the graveyard. If you want, I could drop you off and pick you up half an hour later.'

'Just like that! Enid, I've been dreading it!'

'It's unfinished business,' Enid said gently. 'It might hurt but you'll feel better afterwards, I promise you.'

After a long pause Jane said, 'All right, I want you to drop me off.'

The graveyard was some distance from the village, standing in a fold in the hills, with views of the distant mountains. Jane had always found it a beautiful, serene place. Enid stopped the car and said, 'See you in about half an hour.' And was gone.

For a moment Jane couldn't move. Then she pushed open the lych-gate and entered. Apparently she was the only person there. There was the muted hum of traffic from the main road and the calling of a couple of birds. She walked slowly to where her parents were buried, her sister and brother-in-law next to them.

There were still flowers by the grave but most of them had now wilted. Jane examined the cards, her sister had had so many friends! And she saw a great sheaf of roses—from Jane and Cal, sister and brother. She didn't know he had done this for her! Hard to believe it sometimes, but he was a kind, thoughtful man. Jane set to to tidy the graves.

It was painful, but when she had finished she knew that in time the grieving would end. Things had passed, life would—had to—go on. She walked back to the graveyard entrance feeling a little better.

Enid was waiting for her, placidly reading a nursing magazine. 'You knew that would be good for me, didn't you?' Jane asked.

'Thought you ought to face up to things,' Enid said gruffly.

Jane realised there was an awful lot about nursing that she could learn from this woman.

Jane was now spending as much time as she could with Helen, and Lyn was slowly taking up her midwifery duties again. Things were moving, and Jane found herself feeling more and more happy about living with Helen. The honeymoon was now over—at times Helen could be a naughty little girl. But Jane was happy with her.

Cal had told her he was going to London to see Miriam. His voice had been set, he wasn't going to have his plans altered.

'You know how I feel,' Jane had said calmly. 'I'm interested solely in Helen's happiness. And if I feel that any decision by you will affect that happiness—then watch me fight.'

'I can guess,' he'd said wearily. 'Let's just see how things work out, shall we?'

And with that she'd had to be satisfied.

*   *   *

It was mid-afternoon and Cal was due back in Keldale later. Jane was playing in the kitchen with Helen when the phone rang. She wasn't expecting it to be Cal and she wasn't expecting the sudden feeling of excitement when she heard his voice. But she managed to sound calm.

'I'm just getting on the train,' he said. 'I should be back reasonably early. How's Helen?'

'Helen's fine.' Jane called to Helen, 'Helen, come and say hello to your Uncle Cal.'

Helen rushed over and grabbed the phone. 'Uncle Cal, we're cutting out pieces of paper and sticking them. I've done one for you.'

'That's lovely. Save it for me, sweetheart, and I'll put it up in my study.'

'I'll do you two!' And Helen was gone.

'How did your meeting go?' Jane asked, retrieving the phone.

He seemed to hesitate. 'It was…interesting. Look, Jane, I don't want to talk about it on the phone, it's too easy to get the wrong opinion, the wrong idea. But I need to talk to you urgently. I've got a lot to tell you, things we should sort out. Recently, everything we've done has been in a rush.'

'I don't like taking decisions too quickly,' she agreed.

He went on, 'As I said, I won't be late back. I wondered, when Helen is in bed tonight, if Lyn could come round and babysit and we could go out for a meal together. Take things easy, not be in a hurry for once.'

'Why, Dr Mitchell,' she cooed, 'are you asking me for a date?'

'A date! That's an expression I loathe! No. I'm not asking you for a date, I'm asking you to a civilised dinner at a pleasant restaurant. I thought I'd book at the Lyonesse Arms if you say yes.'

'I'm saying, yes, I'd love to have dinner with you. I'll phone to check with Lyn and if it's OK we can set off as soon as you're ready.'

'Great. I'll phone you when my train gets in.'

Jane felt rather excited when he had rung off. The Lyonesse Arms was the most palatial hotel for miles. Then she felt suspicious. Was he trying to sell her something? Ply her with fine food and wine so that she would agree with his plans? After a moment she shook her head and felt slightly ashamed. That wasn't Cal's way.

But she definitely felt excited. It had been months—years even—since she had been taken to a posh hotel. What should she wear? Her best jeans and T-shirt?

'No, jeans and T-shirt won't do for the Lyonesse Arms,' Lyn said when she called in later. 'The food there is fantastic. But you're also there to see and be seen. Haven't you got any dresses?'

Jane shrugged. 'I haven't needed anything really formal for years. There's a few things in my sister's house, but most are pretty old. I'll just have to make do with a—'

'Let's walk back to my place,' Lyn said, 'I've got a wardrobe full of stuff I never wear nowadays, and a lot of it was…was new. I'd like it to be used.'

Jane remembered that Lyn had been widowed when she was very young. 'But I couldn't take your—'

'Oh, yes, you could,' Lyn said, ''cos I really want you to. You're about a twelve, aren't you? So am I.' So they took Helen and walked to Lyn's house.

Between them they decided that this wasn't a full-length dress occasion—but not a short-skirt occasion either. With a fascinated Helen looking on, Jane tried on dress after dress—and eventually found one midcalf length, in a shiny grey material. She looked well in it...but...

'You've got more bust than me,' Lyn said. 'I think you look very glamorous.'

'You don't think it's a bit...?'

'If you've got it, flaunt it,' Lyn advised with a smile. 'Just don't lean forward too much. Now, what about your hair? That style might be marvellous for being a district nurse, and wandering the hills, but...fashionable?'

Jane surveyed her blonde hair. It didn't look too bad, but 'mop' was the word that came to mind. 'Perhaps if I wash it...put it up somehow?'

'Why not go mad, have a proper cut and style? I've got a pal in the village called Audrey Dee who's ever so good. She'll come to the house and see to you. And what about make-up?'

So Audrey Dee was phoned and duly came to cut, wash and style Jane's hair. Then she did the same for Helen, who was delighted.

Later Lyn insisted on driving Jane and Helen back to the house. The grey dress was on a wrapper on the back seat. Lyn would babysit, staying the night in the spare bedroom next to Helen's.

'Have a good time,' she said. 'I mean, have a really good time. You're entitled to one.'

'This is just the two of us going to talk about Helen's future,' Jane said. 'It might even be bad news.'

'No chance. Cal wouldn't take you out just to give you bad news. He's got more style than that, I know him.'

Jane hoped that Lyn was right.

She had her bath, carefully protecting her hair, then put on make-up and her borrowed dress. She was sitting on the edge of her bed, fully ready, when she heard Cal's car drive up. She wouldn't go out to meet him, she would wait.

He tapped on her door.

'Just getting ready,' she called. 'See you downstairs in exactly twenty minutes.'

She heard him laugh. 'Just time for me to bathe and change.'

So she waited ten minutes, had a last look at her hair and make-up, touched perfume to her wrists and neck and went into the hall. She had to admit it, her heart was thumping. She wanted him to find her attractive. She didn't know what was coming but she felt an odd combination of apprehension and excitement.

Then something caught her eye, something she hadn't noticed when she'd come in with Lyn earlier. On the panelled wall of the hall two pictures had appeared, two pen-and-ink drawings of the Lakeland fells. She recognised them at once—the Wainwright originals that Cal had said he owned. They looked so right against the richness of the dark wood. One was of the great sweep of Crinkle Crags. There was the path that she had—

'Jane?'

Somehow Cal had come down the stairs without her hearing, and was standing behind her. She turned and was highly gratified by the stunned expression on his face.

'Jane, you look absolutely gorgeous! What's happened to the girl in jeans and T-shirt?'

'It's still me. Plain Jane underneath it all.'

'Never plain Jane. And your hair!'

'A friend of Lyn's came to cut and style it,' she explained. 'I thought, since we were going out together and... Anyway, you don't look too bad yourself. What happened to the rather staid doctor?'

'It is summer after all. We have to do what we can.'

He was dressed in a lightweight fawn suit, with a darker shirt and tie. She thought she had never seen him look so smart. 'You look positively…debonair,' she said.

He flinched. 'I suppose that is a compliment. But it makes me think of Maurice Chevalier thanking God for little girls. What you do think of my pictures?'

'They're wonderful. They make this hall into a really attractive place. Did you put them here because I suggested it?'

'Why else would I do it? Now, let's go and kiss our niece goodnight and then go out to dinner.'

'Are you going to tell me about your trip to London?' Jane asked as they drove away from Cal's house.

'Not yet. It's a beautiful summer evening, I suggest we just enjoy the scenery and be glad we're not there now. We'll talk later.'

She had to be content with that.

The Lyonesse Arms was in a village about eight miles from Keldale. Jane had heard of it but had never visited it. It was an old converted Victorian house, with a large car park cleverly hidden in the shrubbery. Not only was there good food, there were fantastic views. The hotel was in all the good food guides, people came from all over England to dine there. Locals only came on special occasions.

As Jane might have guessed, Cal was a friend of the manager. He greeted them in person and took them into the bar for a sherry before they were led through to their table.

'A beautiful evening,' the manager murmured. 'I've seated you almost outside where you can enjoy the view.'

They were shown to a glass-walled room with vines growing along one wall. There was indeed a view, they could just see the tip of Lake Windermere shining in the distance. They were settled, given a menu and a wine-list.

Jane looked at the menu and blinked. Such a choice, and all seeming so delicious! This was going to be very hard. She could put off choosing dessert as there would be a sweet trolley. Should she start with safe smoked salmon, or the rather exciting-sounding fruit and seafood salad? She wouldn't have a steak—there had been so many wonderful ones in America—but what was a Barnsley chop? Or how about squid risotto? Well if it was all delicious, she couldn't go wrong, so she made up her mind and ordered.

Cal also ordered, asked for a bottle of Rioja. The wine came, was tasted and poured, and then they were alone for a moment. 'Now, tell me about London,' she commanded.

He sighed. 'I think I've brought you good news,' he said. 'But I've had a hard couple of days. I would just like to eat our meal in a civilised fashion, as if we were here purely for the pleasure of each other's company.'

'Well, that's why we are here,' she said. 'Just for pleasure. OK, business postponed.' She sipped her wine and smiled. 'This is a really good wine. Did I tell you I worked in the grape-growing area of North California for a while? The Napa Valley? I got to appreciate good wine there.'

As they chatted she thought that it was the most relaxed, pleasant time she had ever had with Cal. Partly it was the food and surroundings, partly it was the fact that she felt attractive, mostly it was because they were realising that had so much in common. He was also a very keen walker and climber, though he climbed less now than he once had. He was interested to hear her describe the walks in Tuolumne Meadows in Yosemite National Park, the climbs on the majestic walls.

In his turn he told her of a few local walks she hadn't yet done, and they agreed that when time allowed, they would go on a couple together. And in time the wonderful meal was over, and they were invited to sit on the veranda and watch the setting sun with their coffee.

He had a small brandy with his coffee, she didn't want one. They were almost alone in their little corner, the nearest couple some distance away. She looked over the garden and the gentler hills beyond. This was so peaceful, so beautiful. But when she glanced at him she saw the stone face that served to conceal what he was thinking. He was nervous. Why? She'd have to help him.

'Business now,' she said. 'You're looking...not exactly nervous but a little uneasy. There's no need. That meal was so marvellous that I'd agree to anything. Well, almost anything. How did it go with Miriam?'

'Hmm. Miriam. A very ambitious woman, you know. She has a good job in London, and though she doesn't like the capital much, she has definite prospects down there. I took her for a meal and we had a long talk.'

Jane thought Cal wasn't enjoying telling this story, though he was obviously trying to be fair.

'I told her a bit about you, she already knew about Helen. I said I was offering her a job as joint housekeeper and nanny. At a very good salary, incidentally, more than she'd earn as a nurse. She said she knew I was relying on her, she wanted to take the job. She wanted to work for—or with me. But I had to realise that she had to think of herself. She was no longer a young woman. She thought I was a wonderful man, we had a lot in common, and in the past we'd had a very exciting relationship. What was our new relationship to be?'

'A very good question,' Jane said cheerfully. 'The two of you, living in the same house, both attractive. Guess what people would say.'

Cal looked at her disapprovingly. 'I said she would be in my employ so naturally I would treat her properly. I was sorry that she felt the need to ask.'

He paused.

'And?' said Jane, now perfectly sure that the conversation was going her way.

Cal looked uncomfortable. 'She said what if she didn't want to be treated properly? She knew we both had feelings for each other so why shouldn't we acknowledge them? She reached over and held my hand. She said I knew what would inevitably happen—perhaps it was best if we got engaged.'

Now he looked enraged. 'Jane, you were right! She wanted to marry me! Worse than that, she expected to marry me! She thought I wouldn't be able to say no.'

Jane just had to giggle, his horror was so obvious. 'I told you she was a very manipulative woman. I remember at school when she was a prefect, she got a new little teacher running round doing everything that she said— or suggested. She thought she had you where she wanted you. It was all she ever wanted, to marry a doctor.' A sudden shocking thought hit her. 'You didn't say yes, did you?'

'D'you think I'm mad? Of course not.'

'And so Miriam said…?'

'Miriam Watts is not going to come and be my house-keeper-cum-nanny. In fact, I suspect we'll never speak again. She wasn't very happy when I turned her down.'

'No one likes to have their proposal of marriage turned down. I should think it makes them feel embarrassed and unwanted.'

'Quite so.' Cal sighed. 'But it still left me with what I thought was an insurmountable problem. Then, in bed last night, the solution came to me.'

'Solution?' she asked.

'To my problem. Finding the right home and family for Helen. It's simple really, I should have thought of it before. I know I've always said I've been against the idea, but I could come round. It's so simple. You can stay here and marry me.'

'I'm sorry. What did you say?'

'I said you can stay and marry me.'

'That's what I thought you said. D'you think I could change my mind? I would like a brandy after all. A large one, please.'

He frowned at her as he waved to the nearest waiter.

Jane took a large sip from her drink, and shuddered. She seldom drank spirits.

'You want to marry me to provide a home for Helen?' she said.

'Yes. I've thought about it. It'd be no big thing, just a registry office ceremony, then we can look after Helen together. There'll be no difficulty to the two of us adopting her, we'd be an ideal couple. Then in a few years, when she's older, if you want to go off on your travels again, I'm sure I'll be able to cope.' He looked at her thoughtfully. 'You don't seem to think much of the idea.'

'It takes some getting used to,' she said.

'It's got a lot going for it. Think about it carefully.'

'I'm thinking, how I'm thinking.'

Jane took another large sip, and realised that she wasn't doubtful, or annoyed, or angry—she was furious.

'I can see that this idea has a lot going for it for Helen,' she said. 'I can see it has a lot going for it for you. But what about me?' She couldn't help it, her voice grew scornful. 'I suppose you think this is a great sacrifice on your part, given your views and experience of marriage. But what about my sacrifice? If I ever get married I want it to be in St Luke's church, with all my friends turning out. I want to get married to a man who loves me and desperately wants to spend the rest of his life with me. I dearly love Helen, I would do almost anything to ensure her happiness, but this is asking too much. Far too much!'

Cal's shocked face should have made her feel just slightly guilty. But it didn't. If anything, it made her angrier. How could he have thought up such a half-baked plan?

She went on, 'No, Cal, I won't marry you. I'll only marry someone I love. If we got married it wouldn't result in one little girl being made happy, it would result in three people being made miserable. This is the lousiest idea I've ever heard.'

She had half tried to keep her voice down, to keep her hissing comments audible to him alone. But she was aware she hadn't succeeded, that there were others around them looking on with interest. 'Is that clear?' she asked, more quietly.

There was that stone face that she had seen so often before. 'Perfectly clear, thank you. Shall we go? And shall we agree to forget this conversation? I'm sorry I offended you. I'll certainly never mention it again.' He paused and then said, 'Ever.'

Only then did Jane wonder just what exactly she had done.

They drove home together in frigid silence. When they entered Cal's house she said, 'Thank you so much for dinner. I think I'll go straight to bed.'

'It was my pleasure,' he said, equally coldly, and walked into the kitchen.

She went to bed thinking that if this was what he called pleasure what would he call it if he was having a really bad time? She hung up Lyn's dress, took off her make-up, got into a hot bath and tried to relax. This had been the worst evening she could remember. And it had started so well!

Sadly, she reviewed all he had said to her, what she had replied. She was certain—well, more or less certain—that her response had been the right one. She wanted to marry for love. How dared he propose to her in that ham-fisted fashion? But now she wondered if she should have been just a little more kind when she'd turned him down.

He had asked her to marry him. For the first time she thought about being married, really married, to Cal Mitchell. She realised that if things had been different, if they'd had more time together, if he'd asked her in any other way, then she might have accepted. At times he was an irritating man. But he was also—she had to admit it to herself—lovable.

Cal sat in his study, his tie and jacket on the floor, his feet on his table, a glass of malt whisky in his hand. His evening had turned out to be a complete disaster! And it had started with such high hopes. Where had it gone wrong? What mistake had he made?

The idea had been such a good one. It would simplify things so much if he and Jane were married. He had thought of it in bed, it had seemed an ideal solution and he had then gone to sleep happy. And slowly, as he considered Jane's reaction, he realised where he had gone wrong.

He had been deceiving himself. Saying he wanted to marry Jane as a matter of convenience had been an excuse. He wanted to marry her because he... Even now he couldn't bring himself to acknowledge the idea. He wanted to marry Jane because he had a...great regard for her. Now he recognised that her picture of an ideal marriage, with the friends, the ceremony at St Luke's, was perhaps what he would like, too. But he had been afraid of being hurt again, had hidden behind the hard exterior that he had developed since Fiona had left him.

Now what? He poured himself another drink. Jane had made it abundantly clear that she didn't want to marry him. He had promised that he never would mention the subject again. He would keep his word. But it hurt.

Breakfast next morning was a strained affair. Lyn joined them, of course, and they had to pretend in front of her and Helen that all was well. But there was a distinct atmosphere and Lyn carefully didn't ask about their evening. Then Cal said that he could do with getting to work early, quickly kissed Helen and dashed out. Lyn raised her eyebrows but said nothing. Five minutes later the phone rang. It was Eunice Padgett, the practice manager. Could Jane call round at her office as soon as possible? It wasn't going to be too bad news, Jane decided, as Eunice had sounded quite cheerful. She went round at once.

'Like all practices, this one lurches from crisis to crisis,' Eunice said happily, 'but something always seems to turn up. Cal says you're willing to work-share with Enid. Enid is happy with that, so is the rest of the practice. So we're offering you a job, for six months at first. Then either side can back out.' She pushed a piece of paper across her desk. 'Here's the contract I've drawn up. Read it, think about it and ask me any questions you like.'

'I know Cal suggested this,' Jane said, 'but are you sure he's still keen?'

Eunice looked surprised. 'Of course he is,' she said. 'He reminded me yesterday, and asked me this morning how things were progressing. He said he'd like things settled, for you to start quickly.' Eunice reached in a drawer for another piece of paper. 'He also asked me if you'd like to move into the vacant house next to Lyn. He wanted me to ask as he didn't want you to think you were being pushed out of his house. You can stay there as long as you like. Of course, Helen would stay with him, but this would give you a little independence.'

'That's thoughtful of him,' Jane said slowly. 'Perhaps it would be better if I had my own base.'

'You'll notice that we're not officially talking about Helen. We've got her in mind, but this agreement must be a purely professional one.'

'I agree that's best.' Jane frowned. 'Could I have a minute to think about things? And I don't suppose there's any chance of my speaking to Cal? Just for a second?'

Eunice smiled and reached for the phone. 'I'll slip you in after the next patient.'

Two minutes later Jane was shown into his consulting room. He looked up, as stony-faced as ever.

'Eunice has offered me a part-time post,' Jane said, 'I just wanted to be certain that you want to go ahead with that plan.'

'I do. I know that you have what you think are the best interests of Helen at heart, and I appreciate that sincerity. You want to be with her—perhaps this is the best way for a while. We must both think of her. For the moment our own feelings are unimportant.'

'Quite,' she agreed, equally stiffly. 'There's no need for me to look through the contract, I know it will be satisfactory.'

'Tell Eunice that. Are you going to move into the house next to Lyn?'

'As soon as possible. But could you keep my bedroom available in case I have to babysit? I'll try not to get in your way.'

For a moment that silenced him. Then he said quietly, 'Of course I'll keep the bedroom available. And you've never got in my way.' He took a set of keys from his desk, pushed them over to her. 'The keys to your sister's house. The house you'll move into has only minimal furnishings. I suggest you go to your sister's and take as much from there as you need.'

'I couldn't do that!'

'Why not? Think of her and remember. You know very well that this is exactly what she would have wanted. Better you than a charity shop.'

Cold words, but she knew they made sense. 'All right. I'll go round and have another look.'

'You might want to look through the photograph albums again,' he said. 'Who knows what you might find?' She almost thought there was a touch of humour in his voice.

'I'll certainly want to store them,' she said.

There was one thing left to say. 'I'll try to move into the house this afternoon. I need to start my life there. I'll be living partly there, partly in your house to be with Helen. And in time I'd like a bedroom for her in my house. But I've stayed with you for the past few days, and I want you to know that…that I was grateful for the hospitality…and that…that I've enjoyed staying with you.'

For a moment Cal's stern expression changed. 'It's been lovely having you, Jane,' he said quietly. 'It really has.'

'I'll go and sign that contract.' Jane fled.

CHAPTER SIX

JANE wasn't going out with Enid this morning as Eunice needed to negotiate her new terms of employment, so Jane went back to play with Helen and to see Lyn. 'I'm going to be your new neighbour,' she said. 'I want to move in at once.'

'Great! There's no one I'd rather be next door to. Now, tell me how your evening went.'

Jane sighed. 'Don't ask. Just don't ask. It was a total, complete, irretrievable disaster.'

Lyn looked at her with knowing eyes. 'There's a lot of love in that man,' she said. 'I've seen it with Helen.'

'There may be a lot of love in him. The problem is getting it out. Now I've got the keys, do you want to bring Helen and look around the house with me?'

'Love to. You obviously don't want to talk about Cal now, but if you ever need a friendly ear, I'm available.' Lyn paused for a moment then said quietly, 'I've been in love, you know.' Then her voice altered and she said cheerfully, 'Let's go down the road and home-make. Planning is fun!'

The house was very similar to Lyn's. It had been well converted, was obviously regularly cleaned, the windows opened and a fire lit. 'Mrs Changer,' Lyn explained. 'Cal gets her to come once a week.'

The furnishings were good but minimal—residents were obviously expected to bring some things of their own. 'Cal said that I should take things from my sister's house,' Jane said. 'I feel a bit funny about it.'

Lyn was positive. 'Do it! Best for all concerned—not least your sister's memory. Go right away and get a load—you can borrow my car. Now, let's make a list of what you need.'

So Jane drove round to her sister's house again. It was a melancholy journey, but it didn't hurt quite so much as before. Lyn would have come with her, but decided to stay with Helen as they both agreed that taking Helen wasn't a good idea.

This time Jane took all the contents of her own cupboard. Then there were things like sheets, pots and pans, crockery and cutlery. There were other things of Helen's to be stored. After the necessities, Jane took what perhaps were luxuries—pictures, vases, even a few of her sister's favourite CDs. No way would these things be sent to a charity shop!

Last of all Jane picked up a large ornamental pot from the living room. She carried it into the back garden, filled it with peat from the little garden shed and then dug up a trailing red and white fuchsia that she remembered Marie planting out. It looked good in the pot, and she hoped it would survive.

Then back to her new home. Helen had a lovely time, helping sort out pots and pans, and was excited when she saw her old teddy-bear duvet cover which had been in the wash.

'It looks like a home now,' Lyn said after a couple of hours. 'Anything else you need?'

'If you'll keep Helen for a couple of minutes, I'll borrow your car again and fetch my stuff from Cal's. Then I'm moved in.'

Even after only half a day it seemed odd to let herself into Cal's house. This wasn't her home any more, even though she'd be here often with Helen. Fortunately he wasn't there. As she had done so often in the past, she was moving on.

She piled her few possession into Lyn's car and cleaned the room quickly. Then she brought her plant in its bowl into the hall and set it on an occasional table under the two Wainwright prints. Though she said so herself, it looked well.

She wrote a quick note to Cal. 'Thank you for having me—I enjoyed my stay with you. I've left you a tiny present in the hall, hope you like it. Love, Jane.' She wondered about signing it 'love', then decided it wouldn't be misunderstood.

On her way out she paused in the hall, glanced into the sitting room and dining room. All beautiful rooms, all completely sterile. They only needed a little thought, a little imagination. Some kind of hanging Persian rug on that wall, a collage of photographs somewhere else. This place could be turned into a warm and welcoming home!

It was strange, putting Helen to bed that night with Cal. While they could concentrate on the little girl, all was well. They could smile at each other, pass towels, reach for the bedtime book. But when she was asleep they had to go to the kitchen, sit uncomfortably and talk.

'Thanks for the plant,' Cal said. 'It was very kind. Mrs Changer tells me that she knows how to look after it.'

'You should look after your plants yourself,' Jane said. 'Gardening and so on is very therapeutic.'

'At the moment I have no time for therapy, and I don't see the need anyhow. Is everything satisfactory in your house?'

'It's fine,' replied Jane. 'It's a lovely house and I'll be

very happy there. I take it you've no objection to Helen staying there quite often?'

'None at all. Just so long as it's understood that this is her home.'

Jane decided to let that pass. 'I've fetched a few things from my sister's, I've put up a few pictures and so on. Incidentally, there are pictures there that were…that were Peter's. Pictures of your family and childhood. I thought you might like to collect them and put them somewhere yourself.'

'That's thoughtful of you. I'm not sure I want to be reminded of things, though.'

'You will in time. Memories become precious.'

'Perhaps so. Now, Jane, you've been through all your duties with Eunice? You're happy with the arrangements?'

'I've talked to Enid as well. We all want to keep things flexible. There'll be no arguing about who does what, we're all willing to make this work. And I'm very willing to spend a lot of my time here with Helen—if you don't mind.'

'Of course I don't! And I understand you've been in touch with the crèche in the village? The one she used to go to before?'

'She still has friends there,' Jane said. 'We've been along and said hello. She'll be fine there.'

'You seem to have everything organised. Now, Jane, I won't see you for breakfast but Lyn will be here as usual. You'll be here for Helen in the afternoon?'

'Of course,' replied Jane.

Next afternoon, helped by Lyn and Helen, Jane worked more on her new house. There was a tiny back garden, made suitably childproof, which was a wonderful place for Helen to play.

'I've only been here twenty-four hours,' she told Lyn, 'but I'm already thinking that this is my home. I've never quite had a place of my own before. Tents and rooms in hostels and hospitals and so on, and I've always managed to be comfortable. In Peru I had my own little vegetable garden. But this is mine, and I think it's special.'

'The wanderer comes home,' Lyn said. 'I can tell you're happy by the sparkle in your eyes. Shall we stop for a minute and have a drink? We're working too hard.'

It was nearly perfect, Jane thought as she and Lyn drank orange juice and watched a carefully sun-blocked Helen play on the little grass patch. A house, a child, a good job—what could be missing? She knew the answer to that question, of course, but she carefully kept from thinking about it.

It seemed odd to take Helen back to Cal's house, to sit with him as they gave her her tea, bathed her and then put her to bed. While there were the three of them, everything was fine. Only when she was alone with Cal did she feel uncomfortable.

Then, when Helen was asleep and Jane was about to go home, Cal told her that he'd like her to take him out to see Jim Benton. Enid had said he needed a visit from the doctor, and tomorrow morning would be a good time. 'We'll set off at nine, then,' Jane said, and that was the end of the conversation.

The practice had lent her a four-wheel-drive vehicle as Enid wouldn't need it half as much as before. When Jane picked up Cal next morning he looked tired, he said he had not had much sleep. If she didn't mind, he'd try to cat-nap until they got to Jim Benton's.

'I'll drive extra smoothly and calmly,' she said.

He looked at her with some amusement. 'I've never seen you do anything calmly.'

She felt like objecting, but decided that wouldn't be a calm thing to do.

Somehow he did manage to sleep. She had wondered if his story had been a way of getting out of having to talk to her, but she decided it wasn't.

She had hardly seen him work with patients before, well, once in the surgery and once when he had sutured the face of the girl high in the Sierra Nevada. And he was good with Jim Benton. There was no instant demand as to what was wrong. There was the necessary local gossip, a consideration of life at sea compared with life in the country, before Cal gently led up to what had concerned Enid and Jane. He'd like to examine Jim. And afterwards he told the old sailor that he probably had a kidney stone.

'We'll get you into hospital for IVU X-rays. I'll arrange an ambulance. Then, when we know what we're dealing with, we'll sort out some kind of treatment. And, Jim, next time you're in pain, let us know!'

'I'm glad you took me round there,' Cal said when they finally got away. 'That was well spotted on your part. The last thing we want is an old man trying to pass a kidney stone.'

'Enid spotted it as well as me. She's the one with experience.'

'Quite so. But Enid's never been to an orphanage in Peru. Now we're out this way, is there anyone else you'd like me to look at? Just so they know the doctor is concerned.'

Jane pondered. 'If you're willing to spend the time, there is someone. It's not really medical, though, it's more social. Jenny Lawson's isolated and she feels it badly.' She went on to describe the situation.

'Medical and social are often hard to distinguish,' Cal said. 'Sounds like she's due a visit. I know Enid's extra-cautious when she recommends antidepressants, so this woman must be in a bad way.'

Jenny was really pleased to see them. 'I thought you weren't going to come after you said you would,' she told Jane. 'I'm so glad you're here.'

'I've been busy, Jenny,' Jane said gently, 'but I always intended to come. How are the children?'

They stayed for three quarters of an hour. Jane wondered if Jenny knew just what this might mean to a busy doctor's schedule, but Cal didn't seem to mind. It turned out that Cal had been in the same class as Jenny's older brother, and this fact seemed to give her considerable satisfaction. When they finally left Jenny seemed much brighter than when they had arrived.

'Once I get organised, I'll bring Helen up here to see them,' Jane said as they bumped back down the track. 'Jenny was so pleased to see you, Cal.'

'I know. Not me, but to see anyone. And I think it's a great idea to bring Helen up here.' They turned off the track and she accelerated along the narrow road. He gazed out of the side window, his eyes crinkled against the sun. 'I've not been on that peak in fifteen years,' he murmured. 'It's a great walk.'

'I'd like to do it myself,' Jane said. Then she made a decision. She pulled to a halt on the verge and opened her door. 'Come on, Cal, get out,' she said. 'We need to talk and I can't do it while I'm trying to avoid stray sheep and hikers.'

He looked at her in silence for a moment, then climbed out himself. She walked a few feet and found a wall where she could sit, facing the grey line of the Langdales in the distance.

'We seem to spend our time disagreeing with each other and then deciding that we have to pull together for Helen's sake,' she said. 'And then for a while it's quite nice. D'you know, Cal, I've had more trouble in my relationship with you than I have with all the other men in my life put together?'

'All the other men?' His voice was mocking.

'Well, there's no great number. But I have had boyfriends, as well as friends who happen to be male.'

'I'm sure. So what do you want to say to me? I'm very willing to listen.'

'We agree we have to pull together for Helen's sake. I don't want her being with us if there's going to be an atmosphere. Children are sensitive, they can tell when things aren't right. Now, actually, I quite like you. I know things between us have been a bit…confused, but can't you pretend you like me?'

'Confused is a very bland word,' he said. 'Bewildered is more how I feel. But there's no need to pretend that I like you. I like you a lot. I think you're one of the most attractive women I've ever met. Unfortunately, you're also one of the most aggravating women.'

Jane considered this. He thought she was one of the most attractive women he had ever met. That made her feel warm inside. But aggravating? Was she an aggravating woman?

He went on, 'I suppose I have been behaving badly. I've not been very used to women in a social setting since I parted from my wife.'

Jane nodded slowly. 'And I suppose my attitude is a bit excessive at times. So now we understand each other, we're going to be friends now?'

'Till the next big fight.' He grinned. 'Shall we shake hands or shall we kiss and make up?'

'I think kiss,' she said, 'but just on the cheek.' He wanted to kiss her. She was amazed how hard it was to keep her voice casual.

Cal held her by her upper arms, bent and deliberately kissed her on each cheek. She could feel his nearness, the warmth of his hands, smell his aftershave and his tweed jacket. It was only a quick, casual moment but it seemed to last for so long. Just as she felt him moving away from her she leaned forward, kissed him quickly on the lips. 'I was lying about the cheek,' she whispered.

They gazed at each other. By mutual unspoken consent they decided to say no more.

'How long since you've been on a long walk?' she asked after a while.

He seemed glad to change the subject. 'Not for too long. Not since I picked you up at the camp in the Sierra.'

'Nor me. We've been through a lot since that time. Perhaps we both need some rest and recuperation time. How about a walk together?'

He looked delighted. 'That would be great. We'll check back at the surgery but I think we could have a full half-day together the day after tomorrow. Maybe Lyn could babysit.'

'We can get to know each other. A bonding exercise,' she suggested, and was tickled by his look of disgust.

'I want none of that pseudo-sociological claptrap. All we're going to do is relax and enjoy ourselves. Where d'you fancy going?'

'You probably know the mountains better than I do now. You choose.'

'Right. We'll set off at one o'clock. I'll drive and bring the gear, you make a couple of sandwiches.'

'Sounds great. Shall we drive back now?' Jane felt better than she had done in days.

She had a couple more calls to make, but they were near the surgery so she dropped Cal off there first. Then she went to the house and talked to Lyn.

'We're friends again now,' she said, 'and I feel a lot better. In fact, we're going on a walk together the day after tomorrow.'

'I'm glad about that. But I didn't think that you'd stay enemies for long. I saw the way he was looking at you when you were playing with Helen the other day.'

Jane was interested. 'How was he looking at me? What d'you mean?'

'Well, he was looking at you as if he was baffled,' Lyn said.

'Baffled?' Jane considered that. 'Yes, that'd be it,' she said.

Jane was surprised at how much she was looking forward to going out with Cal. She tried to tell herself that it was just the prospect of a good walk, but basically she was honest with herself. It was Cal who was the attraction.

It seemed odd to put her climbing kit on again, the boots, the breeches, the good shirt and anorak. It was even better to see him similarly dressed. He looked great in whatever he wore.

She looked at the rucksack he carried. 'That seems a bit full for a half-day trip,' she commented. 'What are you carrying?'

He shrugged. 'There are so many idiots on the mountains these days that I always bring along a full first-aid kit. And I've packed my wet-weather clothes. Have you?'

She sniffed. 'These are my mountains, too,' she

pointed out. 'I've been walking here for years. Where are we going?'

He offered her the map case he carried round his neck. 'We don't have too much time so I thought we might park by Tilberthwaite Gyhll, walk up Wetherlam and then hook back towards Coniston. Know the route?'

'I've done it before. A good circular walk. I'm looking forward to it.'

He glanced at the sky. 'But not the best weather we've ever had.'

After a long procession of sunny days, things had changed. The sky was grey, murky, a typical Lake District day. Jane felt at home.

They chatted amiably as they drove for half an hour before turning up to Tilberthwaite. She was feeling so much happier with their new-found relationship. It was easy to park by the bottom of the old mine and they were soon walking steadily upwards through the great piles of slate.

'Are you trying to hold back because of me?' she said after a while. 'If you want to increase the pace a little, I think that my poor weak female form might just be able to cope with it.'

He grinned. 'I should have known I couldn't put any-thing over you.' He walked faster, but not too much. A good steady pace that would eat away the miles.

They reached the top of the mines, saw the green slopes leading to the proud head of Wetherlam above them. 'I love being away,' she told him. 'Some other country, or even continent. But when I see something like this, I wonder why I bother.'

'It's the urge to see what's on the other side of the hill. It's human curiosity, everyone has it. It's the urge to interfere, to see if you can make things just a bit better.

You have to reconcile it with the knowledge that things are pretty good as they are.'

She looked at him with interest. 'You're a philosopher,' she said.

'Aren't all doctors and nurses philosophers? We deal so much with birth, suffering, dying, the extremes of emotion, it's only natural that we should try to make sense of them, decide what they mean. It leads you to examine your own motives and feelings.' Suddenly Cal looked bleak. 'And that's not always healthy.'

She had never heard him reveal himself so much. Many of his thoughts, his emotions had been hidden. Now she was realising that there were depths to him that she hadn't suspected. She wanted to ask him more, but decided not to. He was already looking a little uncomfortable, as if he'd said more than he'd intended. So she changed the subject, though she knew she would have to come back to it.

'Doesn't the path fork near here?' she asked. 'May I see the map?'

It was a good walk. Finally there was the last scramble onto the ridge, and there in front of them was the next valley—the Langdales. But they were also greeted by a buffeting from the wind that made them clutch each other for support. 'I was half expecting this,' he said.

They had been warmed by their ascent, now they crouched in the shelter of a great boulder and pulled on their anoraks. Cal glanced at the wind-torn grey clouds, now so close to them. 'We're going to get wet. But not for an hour or so.'

'We're equipped for it,' she said. 'It'll be a change from constant sun anyway. Come on, not far to the summit now.'

The last couple of hundred feet were rock, and quite

steep. Jane had to pick her footing carefully because of the wind pulling at her. Just once Cal turned to offer her a hand. She looked at him reproachfully and ignored it. She could cope with this as well as he could. He grinned, and didn't offer to help her again.

Then they were on a wide plateau, with the pile of stones that marked the summit just in front of them. A quick look round at the vistas in all directions—usually wonderful, but now obscured by greyness. Then they sat side by side in the lee of another rock and ate the sandwiches she had brought.

She gave him a bottle of water, with just a touch of lemon juice in it. 'You can always tell someone who has walked in the Sierras,' she said. 'They drink all the time.'

He nodded as he sipped. 'I know. Many British walkers and climbers are just coming round to it. They don't realise what they lose in perspiration.'

She felt at home, relaxed, sitting with him here in an environment both of them liked. She wriggled a bit, felt the pressure of his arm and shoulder against hers. 'I had to lead a couple of walking trips in Death Valley once,' she said. 'With some folk you practically have to force the water down them. They say they don't feel thirsty so why should they drink?'

'And you persuaded them?'

'All the guides tell the same story, a true one. Some years ago a German walker told his girlfriend that he was just going to walk a bit further—up a valley, in fact—and he'd meet her at the top in a couple of hours. He didn't turn up so she called for help and he was found four hours later. Dead of heat prostration. He still had the water that would have saved him in his canteen. Apparently he hadn't felt thirsty.'

Cal shook his head. 'The great outdoors can be cruel.'

He pointed to the sky. 'But I suspect that lack of water isn't going to be our problem. We're going to get it outside as well as in.'

'Let's move,' Jane said.

Their route now led along a broad grassy ridge that gradually slanted down to a path that would take them back to the car. After they had walked half a mile the wind got even cooler and they felt the first drops of rain rattling on their anoraks. They stopped and pulled on waterproof trousers. Fortunately most of their route was downhill now so they wouldn't be troubled too much by condensation.

Then it rained. The odd drops turned into a steady downpour and they both pulled up their hoods, fastened them tight. Now all they could see was a circle of greyness and vague shadows that indicated the peaks around them.

The path was easy enough to follow, but she noticed that Cal took out his compass and checked the route every ten minutes. Good, she liked a careful man.

The route down was now much steeper and once or twice she stumbled in the rain-soaked mud. Then there was a roaring sound, the wind grew stronger and the rain descended on them like an avalanche. Jane could hardly see, it was even hard to hear.

He put his arm round her shoulders, bent over to shout into her hood. 'It's silly, moving on in this. It won't last. We'll shelter for ten minutes. There's a place near here.'

He took her hand, led her a little way off the path and there was the entrance to an old mine working. There wasn't much room. Like so many workings, the tunnel had been closed off. But they could shelter there. They were facing each other, their bodies crammed close together.

Jane could feel rain trickling down her neck and between her breasts. Her feet were already wet, no waterproof system ever worked completely. But she was happy. And she was aware of him so close to her that she thought she could feel the warmth of his body through two layers of damp material. No, that was silly.

She looked up at his face, shadowed by the hood of his red anorak, saw the water on his cheek. He smiled down at her.

'So close together,' he said. 'Is this romantic or not?'

She told him, 'I'm wet and cold, but happy—not miserable. Very happy. However, I certainly don't feel romantic.'

'Romance is where you find it,' he said.

Was it her imagination, or did the arm that was round her squeeze her a little? She looked at him thoughtfully, but Cal's face gave nothing away.

With the suddenness that was typical of Lake District weather, the rain outside eased. He peered out of the entrance and suggested that they move on. She was glad to—being so close to him was unsettling.

They slithered down the rest of the path and reached flatter ground, where they turned left back towards Tilberthwaite. After ten minutes the rain stopped. Twenty minutes after that there was a ray of weak sunshine.

Cal pulled back his hood and stripped off his waterproofs. 'Are you very wet?'

'I'll do.' She shrugged.

They set off again along the now broad path, with room for them to walk side by side. 'I think that you should prescribe mountain walking as a cure for depression,' she told him. 'It's better than medication. I feel good, at peace with the world.'

'So do I. But now I've got you sedated, may I ask you questions? Things I want to know?'

She looked at him cautiously. 'Questions? Personal questions?'

'Certainly. It's only fair. After all, you know more than anyone about my personal background. I told you all about Fiona.'

That surprised her. 'You told me things about Fiona, things that you haven't told anyone else? Why me?'

'Because you were interested. Because I knew that after seeing those photographs nothing would stop your curiosity. Most of all, because I wanted to.'

'Right,' she breathed, not sure where this conversation was going. 'And now you want something back from me?'

'Only if you're willing. Don't feel you're under pressure, that's not what I want at all.'

She felt uneasy, the more so because he was being so reasonable. 'What do you want to know?' She glanced at his face, but he was staring at the peak they had just left, his expression completely blank.

'You're a very attractive girl and you have a personality that is in many ways...equally attractive. Don't say anything—that's an observation, not a compliment. Why aren't you married? Why hasn't some man snapped you up?'

'Not every girl thinks that marriage is the ultimate aim in life!'

'True. But I'm just surprised that someone like you doesn't have a long-term boyfriend.'

Jane was glad that he didn't try to explain why he thought that. The memory of that kiss still burned in her memory. 'Well, like I said, I've had boyfriends—not many perhaps, but enough.' She thought for a minute, this was getting to be a hard question to answer. 'Perhaps because after my training I've never really stayed in any one place for too long. So I've never really had the chance to get to know anybody well.'

Cal's voice was gentle. 'Or is it that as soon as someone seems to be getting to know you, well, you move on?'

'No! Of course not!'

'You're absolutely sure?'

He was making her think, and she didn't like it. 'Are you saying that all my wandering is just to avoid forming a relationship? That's ridiculous.'

'If you say it is.'

She kicked at a stone on the path, watched it bounce down a slope and plop into the stream below them. 'I don't want to talk about me any more. Can't we just enjoy the walk without all this chatter?'

'Of course we can. We should be back at the car in half an hour.'

They walked on in silence. But it wasn't the comfortable silence she had enjoyed before. She felt there was something missing and that it was up to her to provide it. When they were nearly at the car she said grudgingly, 'I don't like being psychoanalysed. But I've been thinking about your questions. I think there might be something in what you said.'

'I didn't mean to disturb you. If I have done, I'm sorry. But I'll go on and ask one more impertinent question. Have you any idea who your ideal man might be?'

'Certainly have. My ideal man is one who walks a lot but hardly talks at all.'

'I'm halfway there already,' he said with a grin.

CHAPTER SEVEN

JANE'S life now fell into a pattern that she found surprisingly enjoyable. She had more mornings out with Enid. For two days she had to go on an induction course at the surgery, so she understood all the practice had to do, how the various elements worked together. There were protocols that she had to adhere to. She learned how to operate the computer. And at the end of the two days she knew she'd be a much, much better district nurse. 'Who organised all this?' she asked Eunice, who was running the course. 'Was it you?'

Eunice laughed. 'Not at all. It was Cal's idea. He organised it but he asked us all what we thought. I think it's a great system.'

Jane thought of the times when she had been tumbled into a job and told to pick things up as best she could, and had to agree.

She saw a lot of Helen, mostly playing with her at Cal's house but some of the time taking her to her own house. And Lyn was wonderful. She was slowly taking up her old job again, but seemed always to make herself available whenever Jane or Helen needed her.

Margaret Claire came round, not on an official visit but a casual one. Unfortunately Cal was out of the house so Margaret and Jane chatted amiably in his kitchen as Helen played with her toys.

'I'm very happy with the way things are at present,' Margaret said, 'but in some ways it's an unsatisfactory situation. Especially as there'll be quite a lot of money involved. No, don't say anything!' She raised a defensive hand. 'I know the last thing you or Cal are interested in is the money. Ultimately, I'm sure we can convince the court of that.'

She looked at Jane thoughtfully. 'I've known Cal a long time. I'm very fond of him. This is nothing whatever to do with Helen, it's just me being nosy. But I don't suppose there's any chance of you and he…?'

'Cal and me getting together? No chance at all.'

'Sorry, shouldn't really have asked that, it's very unprofessional. But I've always thought that the right woman would… Still, it's not my business. Tell him I'm sorry I missed him.'

And she was gone. Jane looked after her thoughtfully.

It was odd. For years Jane hadn't had a home, now she seemed to have two. She split her time between her own house and Cal's, and felt equally at home in both. Often she took Helen to her own house, but she knew that when he could, Cal would sneak a few minutes from work and come over to see his niece. He also seemed pleased to see Jane.

And Helen was slowly introduced to the crèche in the village. She remembered her old friends and fitted in straight away. 'I think that child is the most stable of all of us,' Jane said to Cal.

It was one evening. Cal had read a story to Helen and she had just gone to sleep. Now Jane was ironing in the kitchen and Cal had made her a cup of tea.

'I never thought of you as unstable,' he said, 'but the shock of…of everything probably had an effect on all of us that we didn't realise. How d'you feel now? How are you getting on with Helen?'

Her voice was sharp. 'Are you asking me if I want to go wandering again? 'Cos the answer is no.'

He opened his arms in surrender. 'That was never my question. When you first came here you were full of pity and horror. Helen was the orphaned mite. What is she to you now?'

Jane realised that this was a good question, she would have to answer it. After a moment's thought, she said, 'You're right about how I felt at first. It was just overwhelming, thoughtless love. But now I'm settling down. At first Helen could do no wrong. Now sometimes, when she's naughty, she irritates me. It's a deeper, more complex relationship. I'm turning into a mother.'

'Very healthy,' he said dryly. 'I can sympathise.'

She dropped a freshly ironed little dress onto the pile by her side. 'Anyway, you're in the same situation as me. How d'you feel about Helen now?'

'Well, I did feel just the same as you. When it happened, I was determined to love her, protect her, do everything for her.'

'And were you looking forward to it?'

This was a question she realised Cal hadn't expected. He put down his mug, frowned. 'No,' he said slowly. 'I suppose I wasn't looking forward to it. I saw my life being altered, my pleasant existence being upset.'

'And now?'

'Now I find I'm getting more out of it than I expected. I like being a father substitute, and I enjoy being with her. It's pleasant even if it's not restful. I like being with you, too. We can help Helen together.'

Suddenly, his voice was harder. 'But, of course, as we agreed, this is only for a short while. Then we'll see how things are.'

She felt the anger rise inside her, but she said nothing.

Jane left shortly afterwards. Cal had sensed her silent anger but, like her, had said nothing. And now he was angry at himself. Why did he always have to say the wrong thing to Jane? Usually he was considered good with people.

Probably, it was a defence mechanism, he decided. Whenever he and Jane seemed to be getting closer, something within him made him spoil it. He didn't want to get too close to her, too fond of her. He didn't want to risk rejection. And if she did set off wandering again— what would he do? Could he manage without her?

Three days later he asked her to stay behind again after Helen had gone to bed. Unusually, he seemed rather unsure of himself. He drank his tea, poured himself a second mug and then talked about nothing much as it got cold.

'Come on,' said Jane after a while. 'I know you've got something to say to me—what is it? It's not like you to play around like this.'

'So much for the inscrutable male. Yes, there is something, though I doubt whether you can guess what it is. Something pleasant, I hope.'

'That's good. But before you start, shall I warm up your tea in the microwave?'

Cal looked in surprise at his now cool mug, and handed it to her. 'Please. I was thinking of other things.'

When he started again his voice was stronger. 'In a week's time there's a big charity dance in Kendal. It's organised by the local farmers. It's always very popular and it's always very good. Tickets are for couples only. We usually have a table for the practice, there'll be about twelve of us. Now I know…the last time I invited you out turned out to be a bit of a non-success. But this will be quite different. Would you like to come as my partner?'

Jane's first reaction was to say yes, because she knew she'd love to go with him. Her second reaction was to say no, because who knew what the consequences might be? They had got their lives into equilibrium, they were getting along together reasonably well, so why risk spoiling that?

But she wanted to go. 'So, in effect we'd go together as a group?' she asked.

He was fair. 'Yes, we'd be a party. But you should know that you and I would be the only unmarried couple. I should warn you that people will talk, even those who know our personal circumstances.'

'What's village life without gossip?' mumbled Jane. 'You don't want to take Lyn, then?'

'No. First, I'd rather take you, Second, I already know she wouldn't come. She went with her husband shortly before he died, it would be too much for her. Anyway, she's offered to look after Helen for us.'

'In that case, I'd love to come,' she said. 'You don't mind people talking?'

'We're together every evening. I'm sure they talk about us already.'

'If only they knew,' Jane said.

He echoed her. 'If only they knew.'

'Just one more question. What sort of do is it?'

'Formal, very formal. I shall be in my penguin suit. I gather you will have to be in a long dress. I think the ladies compete a little.'

'What's new?' asked Jane. 'Anyway, I've got a long dress.'

* * *

The practice party was arranged with typical Cal efficiency. He knew that no one would get drunk, but he didn't want anyone worrying over whether they could have one extra glass of wine. So he ordered two people carriers to pick people up and take them back to their homes. Jane wondered if he'd also done it to ensure that the two of them wouldn't be alone together, then decided that was foolish. They were alone together most evenings.

Jane wondered how she'd feel, going to a formal dance as Cal's partner. As the evening of the dance approached, she found she was looking forward to it. Perhaps in some way they could get over the bad memory of the last time they had gone out together.

She was also now an acknowledged member of the practice. She felt she was among friends, part of the team.

Lyn was to babysit and stay the night at Cal's house, and she suggested to Cal that it might be an idea if Jane got ready there, too. Cal agreed, and put it to Jane.

'Lyn and Helen can help you get ready,' he said with a smile.

'But I stay the night at my own house,' she said.

'Where else?'

So Jane took a suitcase to the bedroom she used to inhabit, and Helen and Lyn came in to help her get ready. 'You don't mind going with Cal?' Lyn asked. 'You said last time was a bit of a disaster.'

Even though they were close, Jane hadn't told Lyn what had happened. 'We're just going as friends,' she said. 'There's nothing more to it than that.'

'Of course not.' Lyn's expression indicated that she didn't believe a word of it.

'Are you sorry you're not coming?' Jane asked. 'You wouldn't want to come, just as one of the party?'

Lyn shook her head. 'Not yet—though perhaps someday. I remember exactly how happy I was when I went with my husband and it would remind me of that.'

'Sorry,' said Jane. 'I didn't want to rake up old memories.'

'No, I'm pleased that you do. I can still feel the horror of losing Michael, but then I have the memory of the blissful years before that. And those years will always be with me. Have you ever been in love like that, Jane?'

Jane thought for a long, long time. 'No,' she said eventually. 'Not yet. But I can imagine it, and that's the kind of love I want.'

Cal knocked on Jane's bedroom door an hour later and said that the people carrier was outside. She thought he looked wonderful. There was nothing like a well-cut dinner jacket for making a man look smart. She felt rather special herself, having gone to quite some trouble.

When she opened the door his appreciation of her was obvious. For once, the cold exterior slipped. 'Again, you look gorgeous,' he said. 'That's a wonderful dress. But, then, you always look wonderful.'

'For a man who claims he's not very interested in women, you certainly know how to flatter a girl. So may I say that you look very smart yourself.'

'From you that's a vast compliment.' He handed her a corsage. 'I brought you this. Now, shall we go and say goodbye to Lyn and Helen?'

'They'll be in the kitchen, waiting for us'.

After Cal had kissed Helen and admired the picture she had drawn that afternoon, he turned to Lyn and gave her a small, silver-wrapped bottle. 'A split of champagne,' he said. 'We're all going to have a good time. I want you to open that about ten o'clock and join in with us.'

'I'll do that,' said Lyn. 'I certainly will. Now, go and enjoy yourselves.'

'That was a thoughtful gesture,' Jane said when they got into the minibus. 'You're a kind person on the quiet, aren't you?'

'I try not to let it show. Lyn is a great midwife, an asset to the practice.'

'And that's why you gave her the bottle? I don't believe a word of it. Cal Mitchell, I've never known anyone work so hard to appear miserable.'

She had just finished fastening on the corsage he had given her. It was an orchid, its lemon colour going well with her blue silk dress. 'And another thing. This flower is beautiful.' She leaned over to kiss him on the cheek. But he turned his head. Had he known what she was going to do? Had he turned on purpose? Whatever, she kissed him on the lips.

There was a moment's silence as he looked at her. 'Just a kiss, a thank-you kiss,' she faltered.

'Whatever else? Oh, look, this is where Enid lives.'

Eventually they had a full car and drove to the outskirts of Kendal to Grisethwaite Hall where the dance was to be held. She felt quite excited as Cal escorted her to the entrance and she saw the other guests, in dinner jackets and different coloured long dresses. She hadn't been to many formal occasions like this.

Cal had told her that this was an occasion to mingle, to see and be seen, to renew old friendships and perhaps make new ones. She quickly lost count of the number of people Cal introduced her to. Then there was a nudge on her shoulder.

'Jane? It is Jane, isn't it? Jane Hall? I don't believe it!'

Jane turned. Facing her was a slender young woman,

in an expensive, low-cut black dress. With her was a cheerful young man whose dinner jacket looked like silk.

'Don't you remember me? My name was Annette Richards. I was a year below you in school. You helped me quite a lot, remember? When I had trouble with that crowd on the bus.'

Jane blinked. Yes, she did remember. But what had happened to the plump, shy girl in glasses Annette had been? 'Of course I remember you, Annette,' she said. 'Good to see you again. And who is this?'

'Freddy. Freddy Pawson, my husband. We were in the same class together. Remember him?'

Once again, Jane did remember—just. Freddy had been another amiable lad who'd never seemed to do much, but had upset no one.

'Freddy's taken over his dad's haulage business,' Annette went on proudly. 'We're doing rather well. So, what are you doing now?'

'It seems a long time since we were at school together,' said Jane.

It was that sort of evening.

Eventually everyone went to the tables they had booked and the music started. There was no dinner as such. Instead, from time to time waiters handed round plates of rather delightful snacks. There was a set of bottles on their table, but Jane decided to ration herself. But her first glass of red wine was delicious.

Cal asked her to dance. 'Enjoying yourself?' he asked.

'You bet I am. I'm having a fabulous time. See that girl over there in black, the one I was talking to? Look at her, isn't she smart? But at school we used to call her Jelly Richards, which was cruel. And look at her now!'

'People change,' he said softly. 'How people change.'

'Some do.' They danced a little more.

'I really do like your dress,' he said. 'I can see men all around looking at you and envying me. You didn't bring that back from California in your rucksack?'

Jane laughed. 'Hardly.' Then she decided to tell him. 'It was my sister's dress. I found it in her wardrobe, she'd never worn it. She wrote to me about it.'

He thought about that. 'So you're wearing it as some kind of a statement? To yourself if no one else?'

'Yes, it's a statement. I'll never forget my sister. But life goes on, and the first stage of mourning is over.'

'That's good.'

'D'you feel the same about your brother?'

He didn't answer at first. When they were near the edge of the dance floor, he said, 'I'm getting rather warm. D'you think we could walk outside for a moment?'

Jane felt an odd thrill of recognition. This echoed something he'd said at their first ever meeting, at that wedding so long ago. 'All right,' she said.

He led her outside. It was dusk of the long summer evening now, and lights were flashing on down the long drive. They found a bench away from the sounds behind them—again, as they had done before. Jane wondered if that night was to be played again. But how would it end this time? Then she shook herself. She was being foolish.

'You were going to tell me about your brother,' she said.

'Peter and I were different—we were like chalk and cheese. I loved him, of course—but we had entirely different interests and entirely different lives. Only in the last couple of years did we start to get to know each other, really like each other. And then that process was ended by his death. I feel sad and I feel cheated.' He turned to her. 'Never think that you have all the time in the world to do things, Jane. That time can slip away.'

'So you feel that…'

From behind them they heard the last loud chord from the band, and then the music ended. 'Now we start on the formal bit,' he muttered. 'Time for the speeches. Perhaps we'd better get back. We don't want people to notice that we're missing.'

'No,' she said. 'That would be terrible.' They walked back in silence together.

The rest of the evening was pleasant enough. Jane enjoyed herself. There were the speeches, which were short, and a couple of presentations, which were shorter. Then some more dancing, but not with Cal again. An awful lot of people seemed to want to come to speak to him. And all too soon it was time to go home.

She enjoyed the cheerful chatter in the vehicle going back. They were dropped off in reverse order, so that finally there was only Cal and herself left. When they pulled up outside her house, Cal told the driver to go home, that he would walk the last hundred yards himself. And so she and Cal were left standing on her doorstep.

'I'll just see you get inside and then I'll be on my way,' he said.

She was fishing in her handbag for her key. 'I've enjoyed myself,' she said. 'I'm still enjoying myself. I don't want the evening to end. Would you like to come in for coffee. Just coffee, that is.'

'Just coffee?' There was humour in his voice.

She felt herself getting warm. 'I mean I've got no alcohol at all. But you can have a biscuit as well if you want.'

'I'd love coffee and a biscuit. For the first time that I can remember, I don't much want to go to my own home. Even with Helen asleep there, I'd feel lonely.'

'Lonely? You?' It was the first time she had heard him suggest such a thing.

Jane led Cal into her living room, suggested that he make himself comfortable, take off his jacket and tie. She had tidied away all evidence of Helen into a corner. Helen's toys tended to get everywhere.

Jane went into the kitchen, fumbled together a tray with a cafetière of coffee, mugs and biscuits. Then she carried the tray back into the living room. Cal was sitting in the corner of her settee, his jacket and tie off, looking rather weary. One arm was stretched along the back of the settee. As she came in he rose and took the tray from her, placed it on the little table in front of them. She couldn't read the message in those dark blue eyes. But she sat down next to him.

First she had to pull the table closer, pour coffee, open the box of biscuits. Then she leaned back—and realised his arm was behind her. Nearly round her. Once again she turned to stare, mesmerised, into those eyes.

She could read the longing there, it was unmistakable. And she felt that her own eyes must be flashing the same message.

His arm tightened round her, pulled her to him, very gently. And all the time he looked at her so she could see the need but also the hesitation there. What he read in her eyes only made him more certain. But then she felt that she was seeing too much, so her eyes closed.

He kissed her. Gently at first, the touch only the slightest brushing of her lips. It was so sweet, she sighed because she knew they had all the time in the world. No need to hurry.

He pulled her across him, so she felt her breasts press against his chest, his arms supporting her. She lifted her feet onto the couch, and she heard two distinct thumps as she kicked off her shoes. She wanted to be comfortable. She felt at home here.

Why was this happening and why was it happening now? She wasn't drunk, she'd had three glasses of wine at the most. He had been similarly careful. Something neither of them could account for was pulling them together. She knew it, felt it was inevitable. And now she realised it was what she wanted.

Almost in spite of herself, her hands went round his neck, stroked him, eased him towards her. And for some time they were both content to lie there, lost in a kiss that seemed to go on for ever.

But then Jane sensed his breathing getting heavier, his kiss more demanding. She had to react, opening her lips, pressing her body even harder against him. She knew he wanted more. But she also knew that the next move would have to come from her. Even at that moment she could recognise his respect for her.

'Unzip me,' she said. These were the first words that had been spoken. They shocked him. She saw his eyes, full of both anguish and desire, stare down at her.

'Jane, Jane, perhaps we ought to—'

'Do it, Cal. I want you to.' She had difficulty in recognising her own voice. But he heard the determination in it.

There was the touch of Cal's fingers on the skin on the back of her neck—such a sensitive spot! Then he fumbled, and she heard the strangely loud sound of the zip as it undid right down to her hips. No going back now!

She sat up, shook her shoulders, and the top of her dress cascaded downwards. With trembling fingers she reached behind her, undid her bra and threw it onto the floor. She saw the darkness of passion flood into his eyes and just for a moment she felt apprehensive.

Then his hands reached for her, stroking, caressing her breasts. She shut her eyes with ecstasy as she felt her nipples grow painfully erect. What was he doing to her?

It was now her turn to reach for him, undoing the pearl buttons on the front of his shirt, pushing aside the whiteness and letting her fingers thrill to the crispness of the dark hair on his chest.

With a groan he gathered her to him, covering her body with his so that their naked skin touched with a shock that was almost electric. Again they were content just to lie there, kissing, caressing, stroking, exploring each other's body. She had never felt this way before, so eager to please, so ready to be pleased. And growing inside her was a vast hunger for more.

Now his hands were easing her dress further downwards. There seemed to be such a lot of clothes in their way!

Firmly she pushed him away, ignoring the disappointment that flashed in his eyes. She stood and the dress pooled at her feet. Now she was naked, except for a tiny pair of white silk briefs. She held out her hand to him and the words, so forward-sounding, came out quite naturally. 'We're not comfortable here. Come to my bed.'

He tried one last time. 'Jane, are you sure…?'

'I'm sure, very sure. I don't want to talk, though.'

He stood, she took his hand and led him upstairs. She wasn't sure how or why she was doing this, it was the last thing she had expected. She only knew that she was drawn onwards by something greater than her conscious self. This was meant to be.

She flicked on her dim bedside light. Then, deliberately, she slipped off her briefs and lay on her bed. It had been hot recently so there was only a sheet on it, and her skin reacted to the coolness of the cotton. She lifted her arms behind her head, looked up at him. She was a little frightened—but so excited.

He had shed his clothes with as little thought as she had. Now he, too, was naked. For a moment he looked down at her, then he knelt by her side. Now there was no need to hurry.

She was content to lie there, her arms unmoving, as he kissed her. Her face first, but then his lips roamed, down her neck, onto her breasts. No, she wouldn't do anything for a while, but she moaned as in turn he took each nipple in his mouth and bit, so gently. Then she reached for the headboard, clutched it convulsively.

She had thought that this pleasure was as much as she could feel, but then his lips trailed lower, kissed her where she had never been kissed before, so that her back arched and she moaned aloud. This was like nothing else she had ever experienced, even dreamed of. It was so good!

But this was something they had to do together. She could sense the passion, the tension in him. She reached down for his shoulders, pulled him up to her. For a moment he hesitated, giving her that one last chance to back down. But now she was certain, she wanted him. She eased him down onto, into her and his sigh of excitement thrilled her.

Just for a second they lay there, still together, with Jane wondering at the strangeness, the rightness of it. Then, very gently, he started to move, and she moved with him, in a rhythm that was instinctive, and so right.

They had waited long enough. Quickly they moved to a frenzied climax that swirled her away to places she had never known existed, to a plane of being that was beyond just her, a communion of the two of them.

And it was so good.

His weight lay on top of her, she felt she had never known anything so comforting. He kissed her gently on the lips, then rolled to lie by her side, reaching out to hold her hand. Their bodies were slick with sweat, the faintest of breezes from the open window cooled them.

'Jane, that was...that was...I can't think of words to say it,' he murmured. 'But what do we do now?'

'Now we go to sleep,' she said.

Cal had gone when Jane woke. She'd slept very well, without dreaming, as if everything she wanted or needed she had in real life. But when she woke he was gone. There was the imprint of his head on the pillow, the faintest of smells, his aftershave and the unforgettable scent of a male. She lay there a moment longer, gathered the pillow to her and smelled it again to bring back the memory of him.

It was still early and a beautiful morning, the birds' chorus outside and the sun's rays through her curtains making her feel good to be alive. She pulled on her dressing-gown, and went to find a note on the stairs.

'Last night was wonderful. But I think it best if I'm not seen leaving your house having stayed all night. Will phone later. P.S. You look so sweet asleep. Cal.'

A nice note, she thought. Is there anything missing? He doesn't say he loves you, a nasty voice inside her said. But, then, why should he? Had love been any part of what had happened last night?

She padded into her living room. The coffee-tray was there, the coffee cold but untouched. She took the tray to the kitchen, picked up her shoes, dress and bra from where they lay, looking so obviously abandoned quickly. Then she made tea and went to run herself a bath. She had a lot of thinking to do.

She lay in the bath, hot water up to her chin, mug of tea to hand, and considered. What had happened, why had it happened and how did she feel about it? First of all, she wasn't sorry. It had been an experience more life-shaking than any she could remember. She didn't regret a minute of it. She hadn't realised that within herself there were such reserves of passion, such willingness to… Was she shameless? No, whatever had happened last night had been an act of giving.

So, she was fine with last night. But what about the future? That was different, harder to decide. What was going to happen, what did she want to happen? She knew Cal was a man of principle, would do what he thought was right. The way he had asked—or offered—to marry her, she now saw as the action of a man trying to do what was right. Though it had still been pretty clueless.

Would he now feel that he had to marry her? Surely not. But she suspected that he might feel if not compelled then obliged. And Cal would honour his obligations.

Never mind Cal. What did she want? And then she realised, suddenly, clearly. She wanted Cal Mitchell. She loved him. It was so clear, so obvious. Why hadn't she known it before? She jerked upright in dismay, slopping water over the side of the bath.

She had been attracted to him at her sister's wedding. There had been that pulse of attraction when she'd first seen him walking up the Sierra towards her camp. Ever since then, whatever they had done together, she had been coming to love him more and more. She even loved his temper, even the way he had of getting things about her wrong.

He had asked her to marry him and she had turned him down! Well, of course she had. But now she recognised that part of her anger at him had come from the fact that if he had asked her for a different reason, she might have accepted.

So now she knew how she felt. It wasn't exactly good news. What would he want to do next?

He had told her of the torment his first wife had put him through, of how he was determined never to risk that again. He was suspicious of all women. Right now he must be wondering what he had done, what demands she might make on him. She would have to tell him at once that he owed her nothing, there was no obligation. She wouldn't let him feel trapped.

Jane climbed out of the bath, wrapped a towel round herself and went to her bedroom. She would phone him on his mobile. Only a few people had the number. A call on the main surgery line might be diverted.

'Cal Mitchell here.' His voice was alert. Good thing he wasn't sleeping. Somehow she'd known he wouldn't have been asleep.

'Cal, this is Jane.' She tried to listen intently, to work out what he was feeling from the tone of his voice.

'Jane, I'm glad that you rang. I was going to ring you later or call on you, but I thought you might be sleeping.'

She could tell that his voice was cautious, too. He was wondering what she wanted, what she expected, just as she was doing with him. 'I've been up a while. I've just got out of the bath.'

'You're all right, then? No headache or anything?'

She wasn't going to let him get away with this! 'Of course I've no headache! Cal, don't try to pretend that what happened last night had anything to do with alcohol! We both know that we drank sparingly. What we did we did because we wanted to. Not because we didn't know what we were doing.'

There was a silence. Then he said, 'Yes, of course. I'm sorry about that, Jane. It was something that I—'

She interrupted. 'Before you say anything, or apologise or something like that, I want to make it very clear that it was something that we both wanted. We are both equally to blame.'

'I wasn't thinking of blaming anyone. Jane, whatever else, last night was fantastic and I doubt I'll ever forget it.'

'Nor me. You're wonderful, Cal. If I shut my eyes I can think that we're still—'

Now he interrupted her, but with laughter in his voice. 'Don't, Jane, think of me.' His voice became more decisive. 'But we certainly have to talk, don't we?'

'What about?' she asked innocently.

'You know you're being deliberately awkward. We have to talk, but not over the phone. When are you coming round?'

She thought. 'If you're with Helen this morning, I'll come round this afternoon and we can talk when she's having her sleep. I'll bring a bit of lunch.'

'That's good. Then we could play with Helen a bit and afterwards we can get things sorted.'

She was irritated, though she knew she had no right to be. 'I'm not something to be sorted, Cal. I'm not a problem and I never will be.'

Now his voice was softer. 'No, I know that. You're the most…something woman I've ever met.'

'Something woman? What does that mean?'

'I just don't know. I'm trying to decide. I'll see you later, then. If you want to bring a couple of sandwiches, I don't want anything more.'

She still had her sense of mischief. 'I'll make you a sandwich if you promise not to leave it. Like you did your coffee last night.'

She heard him sigh before he rang off.

Soon after Jane had hung up, Lyn called round. If it was a good day she wanted to drive to Lake Windermere and take her sailing dinghy. She had offered to take Jane sailing some time, Jane was quite looking forward to it.

'What's so special about sailing?' Jane asked. 'You don't race, do you? You just sail on your own.'

Lyn shrugged. 'Sailing is surprisingly hard work. You don't just sit there, you have to be thinking all the time. And I like being on my own.'

Jane thought this a bit odd at first—then realised that she had spent much of her life in the same way. 'I know the attraction of that,' she said.

Helen was as good as gold last night, Lyn reported over a cup of coffee, and Cal seemed quite pleased with life this morning.

She smiled at Jane coaxingly. 'Now, tell me about last night. Was it a good do? Did you enjoy yourself? How did you get on with Cal?'

'It was a great dance and I thoroughly enjoyed myself. There were new friends and old friends and the food was great.'

'Cal's a fantastic dancer, isn't he?'

'Yes, he is.' Jane looked at her friend curiously. 'How did you know?'

'Used to go to the same dance, of course. I danced with him quite a lot. My husband wasn't a keen dancer and Cal obviously was. I'm glad you had a good time.'

Lyn drove away and Jane sat alone and thought. She wondered what was to happen next. Whatever it was, it wouldn't be a declaration of love. Even though she might have liked that, it wasn't going to come about.

So what did she want, or what would she settle for? She decided that they needed to be how they had been before last night had occurred. That would be the best thing for all concerned. She decided to tell him that— unless he came up with something better.

She made the sandwiches and set off for Cal's house. She found him sitting in the garden, helping Helen to plant a flower. Helen looked up, shouted, 'Auntie Jane,' and ran to her. Jane picked up her niece, hugged her as she always did and then had to meet Cal's gaze.

She tried to be casual. 'Hi, Cal, good to see you.'

'It's good of you to come.'

It was warm again, and he was dressed coolly, his usual outfit of chinos and T-shirt. His clothes outlined his body, showed the muscles of chest, arms and thighs, those muscles she has seen... She blushed. She would try to find refuge in work.

'Time for lunch,' she said. 'Come on, young lady, you need a wash. We'll clean those hands and face and then we'll all have a sandwich.'

'I'll wash Helen if you want to do things in the kitchen.'

So they ate sandwiches and drank tea together, making elaborate polite conversation. The heat had tired Helen. After her meal she sat on Cal's lap and was soon asleep. He carried her upstairs. Then he came to sit opposite Jane again. 'Another cup of tea?' she asked.

'Please. And this time I promise not to leave it as I left the coffee.' She blushed again.

It was different, more formal, sitting at his kitchen table instead of together on her couch. There was a silence, an uncomfortable one.

'About last night…' she started.

Just as he said, 'We've got to…'

They both laughed. 'It's a difficult subject,' he said. 'I don't know what to say because I don't know what I'm thinking. It's not like me to be in doubt.'

'I know that. But I'm not in doubt and I know what I'm thinking. First of all, let's both agree that last night was nobody's fault and that it was marvellous.'

'I'll go along with that.'

'Secondly, we can't carry on doing it. We can get away with it once, but the second, third, fourth time someone will notice, the neighbours will hear about it and it'll be all over the Lake District.'

He nodded, deliberately. 'Also true. But it would be all right if we were…if we were…'

'If we were a couple,' she supplied. 'Or at least think-ing about becoming a couple. And we're not.'

This was the difficult bit. What would be his response to her statement? He looked at her, and the eyes which last night had revealed so much had returned to their old stony obliqueness. She had no idea what he was feeling. 'As you say,' he agreed.

She found that she was dismayed. Although she had planned on saying this, she realised that a part of her had hoped that he might correct her. But that wasn't to be. Well, she could also hide her feelings.

'We've got things pretty well worked out,' she said. 'I think things are good for Helen and we're working on the practice together. We've got our six-month arrange-ment so I suggest we keep things going as they were before. When the time is up, as we agreed, we think again.'

There was no reply from Cal at first. Then he said, 'So

last night didn't happen, won't happen again and isn't to be referred to?'

Jane listened in vain for some hint in his voice as to what he really wanted. Was he happy with this arrangement? Did he want more? But all she could hear was that agreeable tone, all she could see was that friendly face that suggested they were talking about some minor medical problem. She took a deep breath. 'I think that would be best. Don't you?'

'Perhaps you're right.' Now he seemed to be a little confused. He added, 'I don't seem to be dealing with you very well, do I, Jane? I do try, you know, but between us…things always seem to go wrong. And I'm sorry, because…I think a lot of you.'

Thinks a lot of me! some part inside her screamed. Doesn't he know, can't he realise what I feel for him? But she merely smiled and said, 'Will you eat the last sandwich?'

Shortly after that she went upstairs and looked at the sleeping Helen. The little girl had gone through tragedy but things were getting better for her now. Jane wondered how her life would turn out. She was obviously going to be a beauty. Jane hoped that Helen would never have to suffer the misery over love that she was suffering now. She bent over the cot, felt the tears stinging her eyes.

For a moment she had thought Cal was going to say that he…but, as ever, he had retreated. So, she realised, had she. What was wrong with them both?

CHAPTER EIGHT

OVER the past few years Jane had worked in many places—and had worked hard. She had loved it. But now she was coming to the realisation that the hard work had been just an excuse for not thinking. She had lived solely for the present. Now she was having to think about the future—her future, not just where the next job would be but what line her life was to take. It was hard.

Now she knew with absolute certainty that she loved Cal. She loved the way he looked. She loved the way he talked. When she saw him for the first time, even after only a couple of hours, her stomach lurched. She loved his care for people, the way he got on so well with patients and friends. But she knew there was something hidden in him, some inner core that she had never penetrated. She didn't know what the soul of him felt. And until she knew that, she must be wary. It would be so easy to make a fool of herself.

She was now taking over many of Enid's cases, especially those that were some distance from the surgery. She enjoyed the work and it provided a distraction, stopped her thinking too much. When they were together at Cal's house with Helen they managed to act like old friends, but she tried never to see him alone. And if he noticed this behaviour, he didn't comment on it.

Only occasionally did she catch him looking at her in an uncertain, assessing way. She guessed he was wondering how she was taking things. Well, she was taking them badly. But no way would she ever let him know.

It was now high summer. The wonderful weather continued, the school holidays had started and there were no end of calls from holidaymakers. Sometimes Jane wondered if people left their brains at home when they came on holiday. Climbers, walkers, sunbathers and those who ate and drank too much—they all came to the practice with their problems.

This particular day, Jane was calling at the Lyonesse Arms. The manager had phoned Cal, who had left her a note asking her to call round if she had time. It wasn't an urgent call. But Jane wanted to see the hotel again. It represented quite a milestone in her life. She had turned down a proposal of marriage there. She almost wished now that she had accepted.

The manager remembered her, was pleased to see her. 'It's just no good telling people things,' he said. 'Lucy's a bright girl, she's attending a London catering college. She's just come up here for the summer as an assistant chef. Apparently, in London she sometimes goes to a tanning salon. She thought that would make her immune. So yesterday she sunbathed for three hours in the afternoon and—'

'She's burned to a crisp,' Jane said cheerfully. 'Lead me to her.'

It was a classic case of sunburn. Lucy was lying in a darkened room, hardly able to move, with a violent headache and nausea. Her upper chest and shoulders, her abdomen and thighs were red and inflamed. Jane took her temperature, pulse and BP, decided that, although serious, it wasn't serious enough to move Lucy to hospital. Gently she spread a lotion on the affected parts and told Lucy to stay in bed and drink as much as possible. And next time to use a sunblock. Then she went to see the manager and told him what she had done. 'I doubt it's too serious but I'll drop in tomorrow to check.'

'Thanks for calling,' the manager said. He offered her a box, carefully wrapped in silver paper and tied with a gold ribbon. 'Just a few fairy cakes for your little girl.' He winked. 'And perhaps a couple for you and Cal. It was good to see you with us. I hope we have the chance of entertaining you again.'

Jane wondered what he would think if he knew how the end of the evening had gone, but decided never to tell him. 'We had a wonderful time,' she said, 'and I'm sure you'll see us here again. Perhaps when things are a bit quieter.'

The manager laughed. 'This is the busy season for both of us.'

Then there were her other calls. There was an old lady who needed help washing, a urinary catheter to be inspected and cleaned. There were injections to be given, a bad burn to be re-dressed, a little girl whose mother had phoned in, a skin complaint needing more ointment. And each visit had to have the usual five-minute minimum chat. Her visits were social as well as medical.

It had been a good but a hard morning's work. She went back to the surgery to report to Enid.

Cal was waiting for her as she came out of Enid's room. He was smiling, but she could tell he wasn't pleased. 'There's a surprise for you,' he said. 'Go and look in the tearoom.'

The tearoom was where the doctors, nurses and other staff grabbed a coffee when they thought they might snatch five minutes' rest.

Jane opened the tearoom door. It was a busy time, and there were five or six people there. And among them, grey Stetson on his knee and beaming smile on his face, was Brad Fields. 'Hi, honey,' he said. 'I've come from America to get you.'

Of course, Jane was pleased to see him. She was pleased when he came over and gave her a big hug and a kiss. This was the way they had been before. Her friends in the room were quite amused at Brad's enthusiasm, but when he lifted her and twirled her round she saw Cal over his shoulder and, judging by his face, Cal quite definitely disapproved.

But she didn't quite know what to make of Brad being here. He just didn't seem to fit. They had been good friends, but this was a different place. And she was a different girl now. But the last thing she would be was inhospitable.

'It's good to see you, Brad. What are you doing here and why didn't you let me know you were coming?'

'I've got plans for you, sweetheart, if you're interested. A job offer, no less, but we'll talk about that later.'

'Well, I've got a job at the moment. How long are you staying?'

'A couple of days, no more. I've got further business in London. I just came here to touch base, to see if you're doing anything tonight. If not, I'll take you to dinner.'

'I can probably get away tonight. In fact, I'll be free in half an hour. Where are you staying?'

He shrugged. 'I'll find somewhere.'

'You must stay with me,' she said. 'I've got a spare bedroom.'

'Jane, I'll be OK. There are a lot of hotels and boarding houses around here and I—'

'Please, stay with me,' she said firmly. 'Now, wait here for a couple of minutes, there are things I have to sort out.'

Actually, she wasn't quite sure about how Cal would

like Brad staying with her. She wasn't entirely happy about it herself. But, then, she rented the house, she could do with it what she liked. If Cal didn't like it—too bad. Still, she thought she'd have a word with him.

He was in his consulting room. The receptionist said it was his lunch-hour, he was alone. 'Ask him if he'll see me,' said Jane.

As always, he was polite. He smiled at her, fetched her a chair so she could sit opposite him, said how pleasant it was that an old friend should turn up. But Jane felt that there was an edge to his politeness that suggested he wasn't pleased at all.

'I just wanted you to know,' she said. 'Brad will be staying with me at the house for a couple of days.'

'Of course. I don't think your private affairs are any of my business. It's now your house.'

'It is your business. He'll be staying in the same house where your niece often stays.' She paused a moment and then said desperately, 'And I want you to know that there isn't, has never been and never will be anything sexual between us.'

'I see. Does he know that?'

'If he doesn't, he'll quickly find out.'

'Well, I'm sure you know best. I know Brad was good to you in America, you do owe him your thanks. Before you came we had quite a chat, you know.'

'No, I didn't know that.'

'And you'll be wanting to take him out this evening. Don't worry about Helen, I can see to her very easily. We'll have an evening together.'

'That's very kind of you,' Jane said, gritting her teeth.

Great, she thought as she left the room. It was good to see Brad—but she wished he hadn't come. And what was she to make of Cal's attitude? It almost seemed that he was jealous. The grim humour of that made her smile.

She picked up Brad and took him home. He had hired a flash red sports car—just the opposite of the high, four-wheel-drive vehicles that everyone around the village seemed to drive. As he drove Jane home they passed Cal's window, and she saw him looking out at the two of them. That made things even worse.

Lyn was outside her house. Jane introduced Brad to her and then Brad went to the bathroom to freshen up while Jane and Lyn had a quiet talk.

'How's Cal taking to Brad turning up?' Lyn asked.

'Not too well. That's to say, he smiles and says that everything is fine. But you know underneath that he doesn't mean it at all.'

'I know what you mean. There's no getting through to him when he puts on that careless attitude. Don't you want to shake him?'

'Quite often,' Jane said gloomily. 'But I doubt it would do any good.'

She made up a bed for Brad in the tiny spare room, then passed a pleasant afternoon with him, reminiscing about old times. He refused to tell her what he'd meant when he'd said he had a job for her. 'I'll tell you later.' He grinned. 'You'll be more likely to agree in the seductive atmosphere of the hotel where we have dinner.'

'I'm taking you to the Red Lion in the village. It has atmosphere, but I don't think that seductive is quite the right word for it.'

Time passed quickly. There was a phone call from Cal, saying that Helen was fine and his evening surgery was covered so he could spend the evening with her. 'Kiss her for me. I'm going out with Brad to the Red Lion,' Jane said.

'Enjoy your evening.' How did he manage to sound so polite and so angry at the same time?

She and Brad walked down to the Red Lion, where she bought him a pint of the strong local beer and introduced him to a couple of her friends. They had a very good pub meal, sitting in a corner of the bar, and talked even more about old times. Then he bought more beer and said, 'Now I've got you in a good mood, I've got something to ask you. To offer you.'

'Well, I hope it's something proper,' she said primly.

'It's proper all right, it's very proper.' He gazed out of the nearest window, then pointed. 'Look, I can just see a mountain top.'

'I know. It's called Helvellyn. Looks good from here, doesn't it?'

'Very good. How d'you fancy a year looking at peaks that are twenty-five thousand feet high instead of three thousand?'

She blinked. 'Doing what?'

'My old company is organising an expedition to the Himalayas. Not to Everest—Everest is old hat now—but to a couple of the slightly lower peaks. Some of them haven't yet been climbed, and they look to be much more fun. Right now we've got government permission, we're organising the Sherpa porters and putting together a scientific programme, too. The pay will be good, the conditions better. This is going to be one hell of a party, Jane. And we start in six weeks.'

'So why are you telling me?'

'We've already got a doctor. We want you to come along as the nurse. Now, while you think about it for a couple of minutes, I'll go and get us some more drinks.'

Jane's head was whirling. This was the perfect job, the one she had been looking for all her life. She'd been on mountain ranges in Europe and North and South America. But everyone acknowledged that the Himalayas were the tops. And a full-blown expedition. She'd never get another chance like this. How could she refuse? But…

Brad returned with their drinks. She sipped, wondering what to say. 'It's a wonderful offer, Brad, it really is. But I've got responsibilities now. There's Helen I have to think of.'

Brad nodded. 'I know. I had a long talk with Cal before you came. I thought it only fair to tell him that I was trying to poach one of his staff. He said you were good but he wouldn't dream of standing in your way. I let you go some weeks ago, now he'll do the same for me. If you want to go, you have his blessing. He can cope perfectly well with Helen.'

'He said that did he? Did he?'

Brad looked blank. 'I appear to have said the wrong thing,' he said. 'I'm sorry. Look, I'm not asking for an instant reply. Let me know at the end of a fortnight. I know you've got a lot to think about. Now, let's drink some more of this excellent beer.'

Next day Jane talked to Cal after they had given Helen her breakfast. 'I understand you talked to Brad yesterday, said you would release me if I wanted to go to the Himalayas.'

He leaned back in his chair and looked at her dispassionately. 'Yes, I did. I gather this is something you've always wanted. We'd be sorry to lose you because you've been very good here, but I won't try to stand in your way. If I were younger, I'd like to go myself.'

She hated it when he pretended to be understanding. 'What about Helen?' she asked.

'As I told Brad, we could cope.'

'And our understanding—that I stay here for six months?'

'Well, we'd let you off. This is a fine chance for you, Jane. I wouldn't want to stand in your way. Of course, I'd expect you to agree to me adopting Helen, she can't stay in limbo all the time. But don't let me persuade you either way.'

'You won't persuade me,' she snapped. 'I can make up my own mind and I'll let you know when I have done so.'

'No hurry,' he said smoothly. 'No hurry at all.'

When she had left his room he stared unseeingly at the back of the door. He had done it again! Why couldn't he say what he felt, that he desperately wanted her to stay?

Brad was walking round the village and they were going to meet for lunch. In the afternoon Helen was being taken to another little girl's house for a birthday tea straight from the crèche. Jane could spend the afternoon with Brad.

'I'd like to drive into Kendal,' he said when they met. 'Not only is it a great little town, but there's a bookshop there and they've got some maps and books that I need. Can we pick them up?'

'Maps and books? Let me guess, maps and books to do with the Himalayas. You're trying to persuade me, aren't you, Brad?'

He looked at her, his eyes innocent. 'I don't need to persuade you. I'm hoping you'll persuade yourself.'

She enjoyed their trip. They walked in the park by the river, had an outdoor lunch, bought books and generally acted like a couple of tourists. Brad was a pleasant, easy-going companion. But as they walked and chatted, more and more the knowledge grew inside her. She wasn't going to abandon Helen and Cal. Her future life lay with them. But she said nothing to Brad, as she had promised she would think hard about the proposal.

Eventually it was time to go to pick up Helen from her party. 'Want to drive this little beauty?' Brad asked as they stood by his car. 'You're insured, and if you drive I can check out the scenery.'

'I'd love to, just to see what I'm missing.' She surveyed the red monster. 'It's not exactly what you expect the district nurse to turn up in, is it?'

In fact, the car was surprisingly easy to drive. Once she got used to the tremendous acceleration, it was less trouble than her own sturdy vehicle. 'You're not belted up,' she said as they approached a blind bend. 'You have to, it's the law in England.'

'It ain't in the States,' Brad said comfortably, 'and I just don't like wearing them, so I'll leave mine off.'

'Look, put your seat belt on,' she insisted. 'Brad, it's dangerous…'

The accident happened so fast.

She was driving slowly, taking a narrow winding route through the hills so Brad could see just a little of the British countryside. The road was only just wide enough for one vehicle. On the rare occasions that another vehicle approached it was necessary to drive onto the verge or reverse to the nearest field entrance. No problems, the locals here were courteous.

As she took the bend, she saw the road ahead. And in a split second they were in terrible trouble. The sides of the road here were steep, there was only room for one car. Some distance away, chuntering slowly towards her, was a combine harvester.

But in front of the combine harvester, driving towards

her at a lunatic speed, was a shabby old van. Jane caught
a glimpse of the terrified young driver's wild eyes.

It was easy to guess what had happened. The impatient
van driver had overtaken the combine harvester without
seeing a clear road in front of it. And now they were
going to crash.

Frantic thoughts, options, hopes clicked through Jane's
mind. The van couldn't stop. It couldn't drive off the
road, neither could she. A head-on collision was inevitable. Cal will be angry, she thought. What a thing to
think!

There was one last, possible, dangerous chance. She
had changed down to a low gear. Halfway between the
advancing van and herself there was a half-open gate in
the wall. If she could just…

She stamped down on the accelerator and the engine
howled. The car leaped forward, she felt the seat push
into her back. Ahead of her she saw the van driver's face
change from incomprehension to terror. Would he have
the sense to brake? Apparently not.

At the last moment she wrenched the steering-wheel
to the side and they missed the van by inches. She tore
into the gateway, smashing the gate into fragments of
wood. Now perhaps they…

But just inside the field there was a ditch. One front
wheel dipped into it and the car came to a stomach-
churning stop. There was the sound of glass splintering.
She was slammed against the seat belt, her head whip-
lashing. But beside her Brad had been thrown half
through the windscreen and there was blood everywhere.

It was agony to move. But she saw that there was
blood pulsing from Brad's arm—he had tried to lift it to
protect himself. A severed artery. She reached and felt
for the pressure point in the armpit and the fast-flowing

blood slowed. In a minute she would fashion a tourni-
quet—but how?

She felt light-headed, nauseous, and knew she was in
danger of fainting. But she couldn't, there was work to
be done. Brad might have injured his neck. He needed a
hard collar but there wasn't one in the car. She could tell
he was still breathing, but it was slow, slow...

They needed an ambulance. The drivers of the van and
the combine harvester were running towards her, perhaps
they could help. Then she remembered her mobile phone
and groped in her jacket pocket, and took it out. If only
he was there! If only he... 'Cal Mitchell here.' So good
to hear him!

'Cal...Cal...there's been...there's been an accident.
I've had an accident. We need an ambulance and I don't
feel too good and—'

'Jane, get a grip! Don't lose it. First, where are you?'

'Top of Wintershaw Hill. In a field. I've driven into a
field and I—'

'Who's with you? Is Helen there?'

Helen? She'd forgotten Helen. She wouldn't be able
to pick her up. 'She's at a birthday party. Can you fetch
her 'cos I can't and I—'

'Hang on, I'll phone for an ambulance and I'll be
straight there.'

Hang on. Not much else she could do. Now Brad was
making little moaning sounds. She'd have to tell him to
lie there, not to move, he ought to have a hard collar in
case he'd broken his neck and...keep up the pressure on
the arm. Let a little blood escape, it didn't do to stop the
circulation entirely. But plenty of blood seemed to be
escaping. She had to hang on! The drivers of the other
vehicles had opened her door but there wasn't much else
they could do but wait with her.

It was either a long time or a short time, she didn't know. But suddenly her eyes opened and there was Cal. His voice was anxious. 'Jane, sweetheart, are you all right?'

'Just shaken,' she mumbled. 'But Brad, arterial bleeding…'

She didn't exactly faint. But it was so good just to lie there and let things slide, let others worry about what had to be done. Vaguely, she saw Cal lift Brad's head, slide a collar round his neck. Then it all got blurred again.

There was another sound, a siren. Then she seemed to be surrounded by people, she was eased out of the car and onto a stretcher, there were assured hands checking her body, a comforting voice telling her that all would be well now. There was even a dressing applied to her head. Why a dressing? Now she came to think of it, her head did hurt. When had that happened?

The stretcher rocked, she was loaded into the ambulance and taken to hospital.

She had worked in an A and E department so she knew what to expect. She was examined, X-rayed and pronounced more or less whole. Painkillers would be a good idea. Then they found her a bed and she decided the best thing to do was sleep.

'You're shaken, badly bruised and you'll probably have really painful whiplash,' Cal said, 'but organically you're pretty sound. The doctor here would like to keep you in, but he's willing to discharge you into our care.'

Jane looked up at him groggily. 'Our care?'

'The practice care. Either I or one of my partners will keep an eye on you.'

'Well, thanks,' she said. 'How is Brad?'

'Brad's in a bit of a mess. He's going for surgery but

he'll survive. Now, I'll get the nurse to help you dress then I'll drive you home.'

'Helen? I should have picked her up and—'

'Helen is fine. In fact, she's with Lyn, but there were no end of people who were willing to help out.'

They felt like two strangers, Jane thought. She'd had more compassion, more kindness from the paramedics in the ambulance. At the moment Cal wasn't blaming her. But his voice was cold, remote, and he made it clear that the less he had to do with her the better. What was the matter with him? Anyway, what did she care?

Her jacket and shirt were both covered in blood so the nurse found her some scrubs that she could borrow. Then Cal took her home in his car.

'Helen will still be at Lyn's,' he said when they stopped outside her house. 'I don't think she should see you like this. I'll get you inside and then I'll pick her up and take her home.'

'Good idea.'

'You've got your painkillers so you should be all right tonight. Don't even think of working tomorrow. I'll get someone to walk down and have a look at you.'

'Thank you.'

Cal walked round to help her out of the car, but she ignored his hand and struggled to her feet herself. He followed her as she found her key and opened the door. 'I'll just see you safely inside,' he said, and she didn't have the strength to object.

Once in her living room Jane turned to him. 'I'm fine now, you can go. But before you do, just tell me what's got into you. All evening you've treated me like a stranger.'

He didn't deny her charge. 'You were driving that car when it crashed, obviously driving it too fast. Brad wasn't wearing a safety belt—that was the driver's responsibility, *your* responsibility. I'm thinking that it could have been Helen in that car. You're just not fit to be a mother.'

She could have said that she'd tried, that it hadn't been her fault, but she wasn't going to bother. Let him think what he liked. 'If you think I'm not fit to be a mother, I shan't even try. When Brad is better I'll tell him that I'll go on his expedition. I'll leave as soon as possible. OK?'

There was silence for a moment, and then he said, 'I think that'll be the best thing.'

Cal was sitting in his study. He fetched out his decanter of whisky and then put it back. This wasn't the time to drink.

He'd had a hard afternoon. When he'd received that forlorn call from Jane, it had seemed as if his life had lurched upside down. The drive out to find her had been the longest trip in his life. He had been relieved to discover she hadn't been too badly hurt, but hadn't she known just how he'd been suffering all afternoon?

She had accused him of treating her like a stranger. Couldn't she tell that it had just been his way of coping? The thought of her being injured…it was more than he could bear.

But he couldn't tell her that. It was him, he just couldn't tell her that. And now she was going to leave him, he had sent her away. He must be mad!

Next morning Jane was stiff—really stiff. And her neck ached. Lyn came in and sympathised, said that she would pick up Helen from Cal's and then take her to the crèche. It was good to see how readily people rallied round. But it made Jane wonder just how necessary she was herself.

Enid came round to see her, and was gruffly kind. After she had gone Jane felt tearful.

In the middle of the morning a police sergeant knocked and asked her if she was willing to give a statement. He wouldn't accept a cup of tea, which worried Jane. All the policemen she knew accepted illegal cups of tea. When she explained how she had been travelling very slowly and had accelerated solely to get out of trouble, he looked politely disbelieving.

She made a statement. He wrote it out, got her to sign it and said he would be making further enquiries. Then he left. Depressed, Jane just shrugged. Why worry?

The same police sergeant returned in the afternoon, and his attitude couldn't have been more different. Now he accepted a cup of tea and had chocolate biscuits as well.

'I've talked to Arnold Drax, he was driving that combine you mentioned seeing. He was high up, he could see everything and he's made a statement. He says that yours was one of the smartest bits of driving he's seen in years. You avoided an accident that would have resulted in someone being killed. That young lunatic in the van had been behind him for five minutes, hooting and causing trouble. My report will state that it was his fault.'

'Well, that's good to know. Are you going to prosecute him?'

'For causing a crash? No. You didn't touch him—just one small scratch and he would have been liable. But no contact, no case.'

The sergeant smiled. 'However, I went over that van and then I looked at his papers. We've got him for everything from driving while uninsured to having an unsafe vehicle. He'll pay all right.'

'Nice to see someone enjoying their job,' said Jane. 'Another cup of tea?'

She was still sore and bruised, but after three days she took up her job again. Anything to keep her from sitting at home and brooding. She still went to see Helen at Cal's house, but he usually found an excuse for being elsewhere, so they barely exchanged a word.

Brad was making a quick recovery and she visited him in hospital. 'I gather you probably saved my life, Jane,' he said. 'First by your driving and then by stemming the bleeding. That's quite a thought.'

'Just wear a seat belt in future,' she said wearily.

'Nothing will stop me. Now I've sorted out the insurance on the car, I'm taking the train down to London when they discharge me from here in a few days' time. I'm still going on the expedition and I still want you to come. But I'm not going to push you for a decision. Take another couple of weeks before you let me know.'

Well, she almost had made up her mind to go. But something told her not to say anything yet. She would keep her options open. 'We'll keep in touch,' she said.

That night she went as usual to see Helen at Cal's house. It was lovely, bathing her, reading her story, watching her go to sleep. But it was more fun when Cal did it with her. She called a goodnight to him, went home. Then she sat there, wondering why she was making herself so miserable.

She had come back here because of Helen, and now she knew that Helen would be well looked after. She had grown very fond of the little girl. But no more could she stand the black looks of the man she loved. In a couple of days she would tell him she was leaving.

CHAPTER NINE

FARMER Silas Kaye hadn't been in for his repeat prescription and Enid was worried about him. 'He's a cantankerous old devil,' she told Jane, 'but between us Cal and I talked some sense into him. He's sixty-nine and he thinks he can carry on as he did when he was thirty. He works that farm alone and it's getting too much for him.'

'What's wrong with him?' Jane asked.

'Apart from him being awkward? Well, five years ago he got a viral infection of the heart and the result was atrial fibrillation—his heartbeat flutters. He's now hypertensive, too. We've got him on lisinopril for the high blood pressure, simvastatin for an excess of cholesterol and flecainide to calm down his heartbeat. If he keeps taking those, and he lives a reasonable life, he should be OK. Anyway, he hasn't picked up his prescription.'

'I'll call in and see how he is,' Jane promised. 'Shall I take a few of the pills anyway? I don't suppose he's married?'

'No woman would ever have Silas,' Enid said.

Knott End farm was miles from anywhere. It was right on the practice boundary, a tiny hill farm, beautiful but remote. Surprisingly there was a good road leading to it. There was also an abandoned quarry just beyond it.

The farm looked even more derelict than many. It didn't seem as if anyone had worked there in weeks. The sheep would all be out on the hills in summer but... Two sheepdogs ran out to bark at her. Jane frowned. They

170

looked too thin. And all good sheep farmers looked after their dogs.

The farmhouse door was open. She knocked loudly, got no answer. So she walked inside, wrinkling her nose at the mess and the smell. Silas obviously didn't spend much time on housekeeping. 'Mr Kaye? Mr Kaye?'

No answer. But from upstairs she thought she heard the creaking of a bed. She would have to investigate.

If anything, the bedroom was even worse than the living room. Silas Kaye was lying on the brass bed—and he didn't look good at all. 'Who are you and what d'you want?'

The voice was slurred. When Jane got a bit closer she saw that one side of his Silas's face seemed to be a different shape from the other. This was a classic sign. Silas had had a stroke.

'I'm Jane Hall, the district nurse. Enid asked me to call and—'

'I don't want you, go away. You're just a kid and I don't like kids.'

'Mr Kaye, I think you're ill. You need to get to hospital, where we can care for you. You might have had a—'

'People die in hospital, I'm not going there. And don't you go sending for an ambulance. I won't get in it.'

He was getting agitated so Jane decided to back away a little. 'Well, can I at least make you a cup of tea?'

He thought about this. 'All right,' he said ungraciously. 'But you can go after that.'

She knew she was getting nowhere. Perhaps it was time to call in reinforcements. On her mobile she rang the surgery and was put through to Cal. No problem, this was a professional matter.

'Yes, Jane, what seems to be the problem?' As ever,

his voice was neutral. She shivered a moment, remembering how it could be, then became equally efficient. She described what she had seen, what she suspected.

'I think you're right,' he said after a while. 'It sounds like a stroke. You don't think it could just be a TIA?'

Jane pondered. A TIA, a transient ischaemic attack, was in effect a mini-stroke, and the patient recovered very rapidly. 'I doubt it,' she said after a while. 'I think he's been ill for some time and he shows no signs of getting over it.'

'I suspect you're right. Those arteries of his have suffered enough. And his diet! Anyway, I know he'll not get in an ambulance for you. I'll come out and talk to him. You all right there for a while?'

'I'll try and get him to eat something. I doubt I'll be able to persuade him to wash.'

'Quite. Oh, one more thing. I've just had Arnold Drax in, he's one of my patients.'

'Arnold Drax?' Where did she know that name from?

'He's a local farmer. You know him better as a combine-harvester driver.'

'Oh, yes, I remember now.'

'Anyway, he was telling me about your accident. He said that only your nerve, skill and reactions saved it from being far worse than it was. Said it was the most brilliant bit of driving he had ever seen.'

'How nice,' said Jane.

'But I blamed you and now I find I'm entirely in the wrong. I want to say how sorry I am.' He might be sorry, but his voice was as cool as ever.

'Well, it doesn't matter now, does it?' She could be equally cool. 'I'll be gone in a couple of weeks.'

'Perhaps it doesn't matter. I'll set off at once, I should be there in half an hour.' He rang off.

He could have said he didn't want me to go, she thought, but she knew there was little chance of it.

If she had seen the anguished way Cal was staring at his quietly buzzing telephone, she might have changed her mind.

She had time to make Silas a drink and scratched something out of the kitchen to make him a simple meal. She also fed the dogs, who were more grateful than Silas.

Cal was a little longer than she had thought he would be. And when his car did finally come into sight, there was another just behind it. Cal stepped out of his car and a woman stepped out of the car behind.

'This is Mabel Kaye,' Cal said, trying to hide the smile twitching at his lips. 'She's Silas's sister. I thought she might be able to help.'

Jane looked at Mabel Kaye—a slightly younger, female version of her brother, but with the same unrelenting eyes. 'Hello,' said Mabel. 'Doctor, if you want to look at him first, I'll pack a few things. If he doesn't go to hospital, he can come and stay with me. You can tell him or I will.'

Jane decided to stay out of the argument that raged upstairs. In the end it was negotiated that Silas would choose—either go to hospital straight away or stay with his sister. He was loaded into the front of her car, the two dogs were loaded into the back.

'A few minutes with Mabel and he'll be desperate to get into hospital,' Cal said with a grin. 'That woman is a tartar. I've briefed her, she'll probably take him straight there.' Then he remembered that their relationship was meant to be cool and formal. 'I suppose I may as well go back now. Have you any more calls?'

Jane wanted to say that it was a glorious afternoon, that the sun was shining, the view was tremendous, and couldn't they have fifteen minutes to sit side by side on the grass and just enjoy being together? But instead she said, 'I'll head for home now, too.'

They turned to go to their respective cars, and she heard it first. A call, from somewhere above them. The call of someone in trouble. Then Cal heard it, and together they looked up the road that led to the disused quarry. Someone was running down it towards them. 'Please, please, we need help! They're stuck in the quarry!'

It was a young man—little more than a boy. He was out of breath, could hardly find the strength to talk. Cal made him sit, try to calm his breathing, wait till he was ready.

Jane groaned to herself as she heard the story. She'd heard so many like it before. There were three of them, they'd seen the climbing on television and had thought they'd have a go. They could climb trees, so why not rocks?

'Have you got a rope?' Cal asked calmly.

'Oh, yes, mister, just one. Bought it yesterday at the market. But it broke.'

Jane didn't need to ask, she knew. A clothesline.

'Trev and Mickey, they set off first, tied together, like. They got so far up and then Mickey fell and he pulled Trev off. They're both stuck on these ledges and if they fall they'll kill themselves!' The lad started to cry.

Cal squeezed his shoulders. 'That's going to do no good,' he said firmly. 'Now, come and show us where they are.'

He pushed the lad into his car, set off up the track, yelling at Jane, 'Follow us in your car.' She did.

The floor of the quarry was flat and they could drive right into it. Rising high above them were perpendicular walls of smooth grey slate, which looked unclimbable apart from where they were split by great cracks. And on the highest wall there were two dabs of colour. Two lads, one half-jammed into a crack, the other lying flat on the narrowest of ledges. A length of broken blue clothesline dangled from each still body. As they looked, the lad in the crack moved a little.

Cal took out his mobile, quickly punched in a number. 'Mountain Rescue,' he explained to Jane. 'They'll be here in half an hour.'

She had been staring at the two boys, tracing the route they must have taken, working out how they had fallen, trying to decide how safe they were. 'We haven't got half an hour,' she said. 'They both seem to be unconscious now, but they're waking up. And if they start wriggling, they'll fall.'

And kill themselves, was the unspoken rest of the sentence.

'I have to get up to them,' he said.

'You can't get up to both. We'll take one each.'

'No chance. I'm an experienced climber—or I used to be. I should be able to get onto that ledge and—'

'I suspect that I was as good a climber as you,' she said coolly. 'We take a boy each.'

'But we have no kit! No rope, no slings, no crabs—we'll be climbing free. If we slip, no protection. We fall.'

Jane knew that climbing with the proper kit was much safer than the non-specialist realised. And climbing without it was dangerous—especially on rock which would splinter as easily as this slate.

She turned. 'I've got my boots in the back of the car,' she said. 'I suppose you have, too?'

Cal grabbed her arm. 'Jane, I don't want you to do this. What will Helen do if you fall?'

It was a thought, but there was another one. 'What will I do if you fall?' she asked him quietly.

She opened the back of her car, pulled out her boots, then looked up at him. 'Cal, whether you like it or not, I'm climbing that wall. I'm going to risk my neck. But before I do, I want you to know something. I love you.'

He looked at her as if stricken. Then a tiny smile appeared on his face. 'What have I done to deserve a woman like you?' he asked. 'I'll say it quickly. I love you, too. Now, let's get up that rock face.'

They each carried a bag of medical stores in their car, and took a pocketful of supplies that might be needed. Then they walked to the rock face. At the foot Cal kissed Jane once, quickly, abstractedly. Then they both had other things to think about.

Her route started quite easily, up a crack that slanted across the face. But after a while the face bulged outwards, and her handholds were harder to find. Still she could do it. She was nearly there, just underneath the lad. She could see spots of blood on the rock. There was a fine handhold, a flake of rock that jutted outwards. She reached for it, pulled at it—it was safe. She transferred her second hand to it and was just about to swing out on it when she felt the first tiny movement and desperately grabbed for something—anything else—to hold. The flake split in half, crumbled in her hands and she knew she was going to fall.

Just in time, her clawing hand found a tiny ridge, just enough to hold her to the rock. Her other hand searched, found a crack. She thrust her hand into it, twisted so it stuck. A jam hold. Then one heave and she was by the side of the young man.

She looked over at Cal. 'I'm there and reasonably safe,' she yelled. 'How're you doing?'

'Getting there slowly. I'll make it.' So she turned to her patient, and winced.

Pulse, breathing, both OK. Blood was still oozing from a cut on his head, and he was semi-conscious. Perhaps that was a good thing. The worst thing was his leg. It was bent at an impossible angle under him, both tibia and fibula presumably broken.

The lad was only precariously jammed in the crack. If he came fully to consciousness and started to struggle, he could easily slip out and fall another seventy feet to his death. Jane's first job was to ensure that didn't happen.

A twelve-foot length of blue clothesline was tied round the boy's waist. She threw the spare end round a spike of rock, tied the boy to it firmly. It was the best she could do. The clothesline might hold. Then she groped in her pocket, took out a dressing and with one hand managed to fix it over the head wound. That was as much as she could manage. This wasn't the place to practise skilled first aid. All she could do now was wait.

She looked across at Cal. He had reached the other lad and was precariously kneeling across him. She guessed that he was doing the same as she was, the bare minimum of first aid and ensuring that the boy didn't fall. Cal hadn't been able to tie down his patient. If the lad woke and started to struggle, both of them would fall. Jane winced, and tried to think of something else.

'When we get down we've got some talking to do,' he shouted.

'I know. But we're likely to be busy for a while. Would you like to come to tea this evening? Bring Helen?'

'I'd love to.' Then she heard Cal laugh. 'Jane, are we

discussing our future seventy feet up a sheer rock face and thirty feet apart? And in such a polite fashion?'

'Seems like it,' she said. She was realising that she couldn't hold this pose for ever. Her feet were starting to tremble, and already her wrists hurt.

Then she heard the rumble of engines, and two Land Rovers drove into the quarry just below them. The mountain rescue team. All she had to do with hang on—just a little longer. It had better not be too long.

It was a pleasure to watch the team's efficiency. First of all two men climbed up to her and Cal, passed thick tapes round their bodies and tied them down.

The man who had climbed up to her said, 'My name's Harry Barnes. You don't need to clutch and tremble any more, just relax and hang there. You can't fall.'

She did as he suggested, and the relief was marvellous.

Harry went on, 'I gather you're a nurse. There's nothing more that can be done for him up here?'

'Nothing. He needs to get down. I don't know how you—'

Harry interrupted, but quite courteously. 'There's no problem. We have two teams going to the top of the quarry—they'll lower mountain stretchers. Then we strap these two into them, lower them to the quarry floor and straight into the Land Rovers.'

'Is it that easy?'

Harry grinned. 'I've done it three times in real life. Practice runs? Must be at least fifty. Now, if you don't mind, I'll get you out of the way.'

'No problem. I am a climber, I can abseil down.'

He shook his head. 'Not the way we do it. Climber or not, we'll lower you down. That way you can't be any trouble.'

Jane was about to object, but realised that he had a point.

Five minutes later she was on the quarry floor, standing next to Cal. They were watching two highly efficient operations, the red Perlon ropes dangling down the cliff, the slow progress downwards of the stretchers, a man braced at the foot of each, carefully manoeuvring it. When the stretchers reached the floor of the quarry Cal was invited to quickly check the two. They had to be taken to hospital.

'We'll have to be in touch,' Harry said. 'There'll be no end of paperwork, there always is. But thanks, you two. You know you probably saved their lives.' And then the two Land Rovers were gone.

Cal and Jane looked at each other. 'Not here, not now,' she said. 'We're both in a bit of a state. You will come to tea tonight?'

'Nothing will keep me away. We've got a lot to talk about.'

'I'll ask Lyn if she'll have Helen for tea.'

'Great.' He kissed her quickly. Then he was gone.

On her way back home Jane called in the village, bought a few special items for tea. Then she waited until Lyn came home.

'I've been putting on you a lot recently,' she said to Lyn. 'But will you have Helen this evening? Cal is coming round, and just for once I want to talk to him when Helen isn't there.'

'No trouble at all,' said Lyn, and looked at Jane searchingly. She added with a smile in her eyes, 'Would it be best if I kept her overnight?'

Jane blushed. 'It might be a good idea.'

It was only a simple meal that she prepared. But she

had bought a bottle of the red wine that he liked, and after all he was coming to talk, not eat. Wasn't he? So well before he was due she had a long bath, found especially attractive underwear and a pink summer dress that he hadn't seen her in before. Then she sat down to wait.

It was hard. She had the sense that this meeting would be definitive, that whatever was decided here would be for good. She knew—she thought she knew—what she wanted. If only he wanted the same.

Her doorbell rang. She was expecting it, but suddenly her heart was racing, she had difficulty in getting her breath. She went to the door to let Cal in. He had come at his usual time, dressed casually in his usual way. But it was as if she were seeing him for the first time—the dark hair, the blue, blue eyes, the lean masculine body. And she still wasn't sure what he was thinking.

There was a bottle under his arm, wrapped in tissue paper. He offered it to her. 'Champagne,' he said. 'I thought we might have something to celebrate.'

For a moment she didn't know what to say. 'But I bought you some of your favourite Rioja.' Then she winced. What an awkward thing to say!

'Where's Helen?'

'I took her straight next door. Apparently Lyn will keep her all night.'

He leaned forward, kissed her on the cheek. 'Are you going to invite me in?'

'Oh, yes, sure, come through. Tea's nearly ready, we can—'

'There's no hurry to eat. I'm not too hungry yet—are you?'

She thought about it. 'No,' she said. 'Let's open the champagne. Do we know what we're celebrating?'

'I think we decide that right now.'

There was another little flurry of activity as she found suitable glasses, he opened the bottle, the wine was poured. Then they found themselves sitting on her couch. But she was at one end, he was at the other. He looked at the space between them, looked up at her and smiled. 'I like this couch,' he said. 'It's very comfortable.'

She thought of the last time they'd been on it together, blushed but said nothing. She didn't want to hurry. Things must take their proper pace.

'We could drink to the health of those two boys,' she said. 'Have you heard any more about them?'

'I rang the hospital. Both will be kept in, the one you looked after is going to need some very extensive surgery on his leg. But both will survive. We probably saved their lives, Jane. That's cause for celebration.'

'Then we'll celebrate.' She drank too deeply from her glass, the bubbles got up her nose and she spluttered and coughed. This wasn't the sophisticated image she wanted to present!

Gravely, he said, 'Just before we started climbing you said that you loved me.'

She bowed her head over her glass. 'Yes. Yes, I know I did.'

'We were both a little excited, nervous even. Are you sure you meant it?'

That was enough. She slammed her glass down on the table, ignored the fact that the champagne had splashed all over it. 'Of course I meant it, you idiot. And you said you loved me. Now, are you going to sit there and ask stupid questions or are you going to come over here and do something about it?'

'I'm going to do something about it.' Cal's voice was more than teasing, it was promising. He slid to her end of the couch, put down his glass and took her head between his hands. He kissed her, very softly. He kissed her on the lips and then on her cheeks, on her chin, the corners of her eyes.

Slowly, her body relaxed. She wrapped her arms round his neck and lay back against the cushions so he had to lie over her. This was what she wanted, she wanted nothing more. Everything was going to be all right.

It was so good, being kissed like that. But after a while he stopped, ran a finger down the side of her face, from brow to the side of her mouth, so she bit at it gently.

'I think I've loved you since we first met,' he said softly. 'When you told me about agreeing that you were beautiful. And you were so beautiful. You turned that wedding into a joy for me. And then, very properly, you left me.'

'Not properly,' she mumbled. 'I was being a bit prissy and I'm sorry.'

'Well, I liked you for it. And now I know—I came to America because I wanted to see you again. And when I did see you, my world changed.'

'You were suspicious of me,' she pointed out. ' You didn't really trust me.'

'I didn't really trust myself. I thought I would lose you again. And I didn't want to go through that a second time.'

She thought back. 'I guess I've always loved you, too,' she said, almost shyly. 'But we seem to always be arguing. Just think, two minutes ago I called you an idiot and said you were stupid.'

'Going to be hard getting along together. We'll have to agree on what we both like best, and stick to that. Are you hungry?'

Hungry? At a time like this? 'No!' she said. 'And, Cal

Mitchell, if right now you want to get off this couch and start eating then I'll—'

'I actually thought we might go to bed,' he said.

'Oh?' she said. 'I've done it again, haven't I? Still, it's a very good idea.'

She had drawn her bedroom curtains, the evening sun shone through them with a gentle golden glow. She stood still by the side of her bed as he undressed her, slowly, kissing each limb as it was revealed. And when he had finished he stood while she did the same for him.

'Oh,' she said when he was naked. 'Oh, I see.'

It was warm enough to lie on top of the sheets. There was freedom to roll, to sigh, to shake her head and an overwhelming, insistent need for him that would not be denied. She could tell he felt the same way. And then, quite soon, she was lying with her head on his shoulder, feeling the heat of their bodies together grow less, feeling their pounding heartbeats slow.

'You've got to stay the night,' she said drowsily. 'I want to do it again.'

'Funny you should say that. But before I say yes…you've got to say yes, too.'

'Say yes to what?'

Cal leaned over the side of the bed, reached for his chinos and felt in the pocket. Then he showed her what was in his hand—a tiny, rather battered box. With a finger he flipped it open.

Inside was a ring, a heavy gold ring with a cabochon sapphire surrounded by diamonds. 'My grandmother's engagement ring,' he said. He took her left hand, poised the ring over her third finger. 'Will you marry me, Jane?' he asked. 'Not for Helen, not for convenience, but because I love you so desperately.'

She moved her hand up, the ring slipped on naturally.

'Of course I will,' she whispered tenderly. He kissed her again.

Everything now seemed so right, so proper. 'We must tell Helen tomorrow,' Jane said. 'She'll be so happy at having all three of us living together.'

'We'll all be happy. And in a month or so—when things are settled and we are ready—she can be a bridesmaid.'

'She'll love that.' Jane smiled, and then she gave herself up to the passionate embrace of her husband-to-be.

Modern Romance™
...seduction and
passion guaranteed

Tender Romance™
...love affairs that
last a lifetime

Sensual Romance™
...sassy, sexy and
seductive

Blaze Romance™
...the temperature's
rising

Medical Romance™
...medical drama on
the pulse

Historical Romance™
...rich, vivid and
passionate

27 new titles every month.

*With all kinds of Romance for
every kind of mood...*

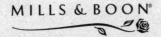

MILLS & BOON®

the
Mother's
Day
collection

Margaret Way Kate Hoffmann Helen Dickson

Money Off
Voucher
see inside for details

Available from 21st February 2003

*Available at most branches of WH Smith,
Tesco, Martins, Borders, Eason, Sainsbury's
and all good paperback bookshops.*

0303/024/MB65

Become a Panel Member

If YOU are a regular United Kingdom buyer of Mills & Boon® Medical Romance™ you might like to tell us your opinion of the books we publish to help us in publishing the books *you* like.

Mills & Boon have a Reader Panel of Medical Romance™ readers. Each person on the panel receives a short questionnaire (taking about five minutes to complete) every third month asking for opinions of the past month's Medical Romances. All people who send in their replies have a chance of winning a FREE year's supply of Medical Romances.

If YOU would like to be considered for inclusion on the panel please fill in and return the following survey. We can't guarantee that everyone will be on the panel but first come will be first considered.

Where did you buy this novel?

❑   WH Smith
❑   Tesco
❑   Borders
❑   Sainsbury's
❑   Direct by mail
❑   Other (please state) _____

What themes do you enjoy most in the Mills & Boon® novels that you read? (Choose all that apply.)

❑   Amnesia
❑   Family drama (including babies/young children)
❑   Hidden/Mistaken identity
❑   Historical setting
❑   Marriage of convenience
❑   Medical drama
❑   Mediterranean men
❑   Millionaire heroes
❑   Mock engagement or marriage
❑   Outback setting
❑   Revenge

- ❏ Sheikh heroes
- ❏ Secret baby
- ❏ Shared pasts
- ❏ Western

On average, how many Mills & Boon® novels do you read
every month? _____

Please provide us with your name and address:

Name: _____
Address: _____
_____
_____
_____

What is your occupation?
(OPTIONAL)
_____

In which of the following age groups do you belong?
(OPTIONAL)

- ❏ 18 to 24
- ❏ 25 to 34
- ❏ 35 to 49
- ❏ 50 to 64
- ❏ 65 or older

Thank you for your help!
Your feedback is important in helping us offer
quality products you value.

The Reader Service
Reader Panel Questionnaire
FREEPOST CN81
Croydon CR9 3WZ

FREE!

2 Books
and a surprise gift!

We would like to take this opportunity to thank you for reading this Mills & Boon® book by offering you the chance to take TWO more specially selected titles from the Medical Romance™ series absolutely FREE! We're also making this offer to introduce you to the benefits of the Reader Service™—

- ★ FREE home delivery
- ★ FREE gifts and competitions
- ★ FREE monthly Newsletter
- ★ Books available before they're in the shops
- ★ Exclusive Reader Service discount

Accepting these FREE books and gift places you under no obligation to buy; you may cancel at any time, even after receiving your free shipment. Simply complete your details below and return the entire page to the address below. **You don't even need a stamp!**

YES! Please send me 2 free Medical Romance books and a surprise gift. I understand that unless you hear from me, I will receive 4 superb new titles every month for just £2.55 each, postage and packing free. I am under no obligation to purchase any books and may cancel my subscription at any time. The free books and gift will be mine to keep in any case.

M3ZEB

Ms/Mrs/Miss/Mr ....Initials...
BLOCK CAPITALS PLEASE

Surname...

Address...

....

....Postcode ....

Send this whole page to:
UK: The Reader Service, FREEPOST CN8I, Croydon, CR9 3WZ
EIRE: The Reader Service, PO Box 4546, Kilcock, County Kildare (stamp required)